Tre Pound 3:

DISOBEYISH

Tre Pound 3:
DISOBEYISH

By

Jordan Belcher

Felony Books, P.O. Box 1577, Belton, MO 64012

Felony Books, a division of Olive Group, LLC,
P.O. Box 1577, Belton, MO 64012

ISBN-13: 978-1-940560-19-9

Library of Congress Control Number: 2015900972

Felony Books 1st edition February 2015

10 9 8 7 6 5 4 3 2 1

Manufactured in the United States of America

For information regarding special discounts for bulk purchases, please contact Felony Books at felonybooks@gmail.com.

"... every citizen possesses an inherent right to decide for himself which laws to obey and when to disobey them."

–Richard Nixon

Chapter 1

Shelton King had been making calls from his office all morning, trying to generate more business. Processed loans hadn't been this low since he started King Financial. There was a reason to it, though; there always was.

He stared at his desk phone for a few moments, contemplating his next move. Then he looked up when his vice president, Kimberly Washington, walked in his office wearing a buttoned, cleavage-bearing cotton shirt and vest. She looked unhappy.

"Fire me," she said, as she came around his desk and sat her tush in his lap, crossing her legs. She picked up his limp arms and wrapped them around her waist, making him hug her. "I'm not doing my job, boss. Just fire me."

"You're doing all you can to try and pick things up," Shelton said. "It's business. You have good quarters and you have bad ones. This summer just happens to be a bad one."

"I'll stay late tonight if you want me to."

"It's gonna take more than that, Kim."

"Tell me what I need to do and I'll do it." She put her lips close to his ear and whispered, "Do I need to overcharge some folks? I'll make it look legit."

That won't be enough either, Shelton thought to himself, as he rubbed her thighs gently. *It's gonna take another homicide to get business back up in this market.*

When Shelton first started King Financial, he murdered Derrick "Drought Man" Weber to get business moving. Drought Man was the main guy moving large amounts of dope in the city, and Shelton knew without the 12th Street kingpin in the game, drug dealers would suffer, and thus families would suffer, leaving them to come to King Financial for loans. Business boomed since the death of Drought Man.

But then another 12th Street alumni, Rowland "Row" Reed, got out of prison and became the new "Drought Man." Shelton killed him quickly, within a few months of his release. Now the word on the street was that *another* 12th Street gangster named Spook was flooding the streets of Kansas City with cocaine.

They won't die, Shelton thought with a chuckle.

"What's so funny, boss?" Kim asked. "Am I too heavy?"

"You're fine," Shelton said.

He liked how quick Kim was to suggest cooking the books to garner more income. She was the only one outside the family that knew of King Financial's international money-laundering ring. She kept a good record of cartel accounts and knew how to hide them. But she didn't know about the murders that helped build the company, or that Spook was standing in the way of a possible record-breaking fiscal quarter. Kim was a college-educated, principled Black woman with 15-years-plus experience in management and accounting who e-mailed Shelton a résumé during a time when he would have done anything possible to make sure his new business was a success. He hoped he hadn't ruined her.

As he continued to rub her and enjoy the warmth of her bottom in his lap, he wondered if he should just let Spook go and do without the income brought in during droughts. He had tapped into other markets since his start and had increased his revenue tenfold. Drought money was good money but it wouldn't make or break him at this point in his career. And there could be a bright side to this summer, a season known to the underworld as "funk season." Alongside the Fahrenheit rising, killings would also rise. The heat always brought out the bad in people, and bad people would need bond money and lawyer fees. Shelton smiled.

"I got a project for you," he said to Kim. "I wanna start a marketing campaign for people seeking legal help. *'Need a criminal lawyer? We got you covered. Need to get outta jail right now? We got you covered.'* I think King Financial needs to let the world know all the reasons they need a loan from us."

"We could probably team up with bondsmen and law firms to get the word out," Kim suggested. "I can make some cold calls and stop by some places in person to get them to recommend us to their customers. How does that sound?"

"It's a start."

Suddenly his cousin Gutta—who hadn't been working here long and who clearly had forgotten about the knock-first rule—burst into his office. He was wearing a navy blue polo tucked in, with a name tag Shelton made him clip on that bared his real name, Maurice King. Kim sprang up off Shelton's lap and tried to pretend she was showing her boss something on the computer.

"Shelton, we got a problem," said Gutta frantically. "The police are outside!"

Shelton hastily slipped his suspender straps back on his broad shoulders and shot to his feet. "What happened?" he asked, throwing on his suit jacket.

"They just showed up in a pack of cars. I told the girls not to let 'em in."

"State or federal?" Shelton asked.

"Federal," Gutta replied gravely.

"Fuck!"

Kim cursed too.

"I know," Gutta agreed. "What do you want me to do?"

Shelton strutted past him and out of his office. Five men in blue jackets with "FBI" printed on their ballcaps were being let in by a frightened billing clerk that Kim hired last year.

"Donna, no—" Shelton began. But it was too late.

One of the lawmen pushed inside and flashed a badge with the FBI insignia. "FBI," the agent said curtly, as if it was a waste of time to introduce himself. "Shelton King, can you put your hands behind your back, please?"

All the women behind their desks stopped working and eyed Shelton with worried and haunted faces. One girl even had tears trailing down her cheeks. He gave them all a quick, reassuring glance as he turned and put his hands behind his back.

"You know what to do," Shelton said to Kim.

She nodded.

Then, as Shelton was being handcuffed, he looked to

the corner of the room at Gutta, who was bravely standing up near his desk, waiting for a command.

"Tell Tre Pound what's going on," Shelton said to him. "He'll know what I need him to do."

The agents led Shelton King outside—and the circus began.

Camera lights exploded in his face blindingly, as news reporters from all over the city blocked the path to the cruiser, all hurling questions at the same time.

"Mr. Shelton King, are you laundering money?"

"How long have you been involved in criminal activity?"

"Mr. King, have you ever sold drugs?"

"Did you murder Derrick Weber, also known as Drought Man?"

Chapter 2

Tre Pound shifted the Infiniti into park and cut the engine. He leaned back in his seat and the fine leather compressed. "You got'cha pistol?" he asked Seneca.

"Always," Seneca replied, patting his waist where his 9mm was concealed. "Why, what are we about to do?"

"Nothing right now but wait. You see that house right there?"

Tre Pound pointed to a house with a brick foundation and shameful burgundy siding. It was a classic inner-city Kansas City home similar to the rest of the homes in this run-down northeastern neighborhood, with its long driveway running along the side into an overgrown backyard. In the front yard there was a tree stump. They were parked two houses down from it.

"I see it," said Seneca.

"Spook's baby momma lives there. Bitch named Shavon. Dominique brought me over here once and almost got me killed. It turned out to be a blessing because now I know where I can catch Spook slippin'."

"I know Shavon. Cash got her number before."

"Are you talking' about the same Shavon?"

"Uh-huh. Her and Dominique used to hang together at school. Shavon dropped out after she got pregnant. I knew her baby daddy was from the Twelve but I didn't know his name was Spook. Damn, Tre, If I would've known we was getting' down today, I wouldn't have worn these slide-ons."

"We're just doing homework, you're good. We're gonna see if he shows up, then follow him to see where he goes. Hopefully we can get lucky and he leads us to a stash house. Once we learn his routine and the best spot to get him, then we're gonna get him."

"So we're gonna rob him and kill him?"

"No. Just rob him. If we kill him, he won't be able to hustle up more money so we can rob him again. You only kill if you have to."

Seneca nodded. "Shavon is from the Tre."

"Really?"

Seneca nodded. "Yep. Cash know more about her than me, though. You want me to call him?"

Back when Tre Pound was here last time with Dominique, he thought it had been strange that Shavon hadn't said a word to Spook, the father of her child, that Tre was right there in the driveway no more than fifty feet away. If she had said anything, if she had pointed Tre Pound out or winked or nodded to Spook, if she had done *anything* to tip him off, then her 12th Street baby daddy would have gotten out of the car and put a full clip in Tre Pound quick. Instead, Shavon kept quiet until Spook was gone and warned Tre Pound to leave before he got back. It made sense now, now that Tre Pound knew she was from the Tre. Shavon was loyal to her 'hood, not to her baby daddy.

"You want me to call Cash to see what he knows about her?" Seneca asked again.

"Not now," Tre Pound replied, as he watched the house.

15

"Why couldn't he come with us?"

"Cash? Nah, too many heads in one car looks suspicious. And plus I need to talk to you about something', man to man."

"Wussup?"

Tre Pound cut his eyes at Seneca. All Tre Pound could think about was Camille's distraught face when she told him that Seneca crept into her room that night while she was sleep. Seneca tried to fuck her, and if Camille wasn't so damn tough-spirited, he might have tried to take it. There was a strange, burning anger inside Tre Pound that actually made him think about shooting little Seneca in the head right now just to see his head smack against the window a millisecond after the blast. Tre could wipe the windows down real quick—or maybe even just roll the windows down and clean the blood up later—and then kick the teen's inert body out the car.

"Did you try to fuck Camille?" Tre Pound asked, glowering at him.

Seneca was startled. It was the face of a boy who hadn't yet learned how to react to a no-nonsense question.

"Huh?"

"Nigga, you heard me."

"I didn't touch Camille," Seneca said.

"I know something' happened. Don't play me stupid. I told you what I do to muthafuckas that try to make me look stupid."

Seneca spoke softly. "She just overreacted."

"Now you tryna put it off on Camille?"

"No. I ... I just wanted to see what she looked like while she sleeps. But then once I got in there, I kinda wanted to see what her skin felt like."

"Why would that even be a thought in yo head, Seneca? Are you having a problem getting' pussy?"

"No."

"Then what is it?"

"I thought you and her—"

"You thought me and her what?" Tre Pound dared him.

"I thought—"

"You thought what?"

Tre Pound wasn't going to let him say it. *I thought you and her fucked so I wanted to fuck her too.* Hearing that out loud might have really made Tre Pound snap.

"If you need a bitch to skeet in real quick," said Tre, "I got one not too far from here named Buttercup. She'll do whatever freaky shit you want if I tell her to."

"I got bitches," Seneca said defensively.

"Do you? If you creepin' in Camille's room at night, you must not. I understand you're at that age where you wanna fuck night and day. You wanna get that cum out of you by any means. But nigga you gotta control that shit; that's part of being a man. You better buy some head from a cluck before you touch Camille, I know that much. For one, she's your sister. For two, she don't even have any titties."

Seneca scratched his knee, a nervous tick. He didn't know how to apologize. "Where we goin' after we leave here?" he asked, changing the subject.

Tre Pound didn't answer him. His attention went to the three cars coming down the street. One was a black old school Buick Grand National, and behind that a blue Suburban, and then another family-sized sedan behind that, maybe a newer Buick. They watched Spook get out of the passenger seat of the Grand National carrying his son. No one else got out. He paced to the front of the house and banged on the front door.

"Something is about to go down," Tre Pound observed. "Spook is three cars deep and he's in a rush to drop off his son."

"Could the stash house be here?" Seneca asked.

"Could be."

Seneca pulled out his 9mm and rested it on his thigh. "Are we following them or are we about to hop out? I wanna hop out."

Tre Pound peered at him and smiled a little. Seneca was a loyal little nigga, if nothing else. Or maybe he was just trying to make up for the Camille thing.

"Trust me, I wanna get these muhfuckas right now too," said Tre Pound. "These are the niggas that shot me up at Camille's talent show. But getting' 'em is easy. Getting' 'em good, though, takes strategy."

Seneca nodded, but Tre Pound still wasn't sure if he understood. When Tre Pound was his age he didn't understand all the guidance Cutthroat gave him until later on in life.

Across the street, Spook was banging on the front door now, and when it finally opened he quickly handed his son off to Shavon like the boy was a package. Tre Pound's phone rang as Spook raced back to the car. Tre Pound put the phone up to his ear, still keeping his eyes on his target.

"Hello?"

"Tre, Shelton just got arrested!" Gutta said frantically. "FBI swooped him up."

"What?!" Tre Pound started up his car. "When?"

"Like ten minutes ago. They walked him out in cuffs. Shelton told me to tell you that you should know what to do. What is he talking' about?"

Grab Camille, Tre Pound remembered. Shelton told him a long time ago that if he ever got locked up for any reason, make sure Camille was safe and secure. If the Feds were involved, they'd be doing a sweep of all of Shelton's properties, commercial and residential. And like Tre Pound, Camille had been staying at Shelton's house the last few weeks. She was vulnerable to a federal sweep that could land her in a detention center.

"I'ma call you back, Gutta."

Tre Pound hung up, then shifted into gear and hit the gas, wheeling his luxury car into the middle of the road in a perfect U-turn. He kept his foot on the gas and barreled back down the road.

"We gotta get Camille," Tre Pound said, pushing the Infiniti faster. "Reach in the back seat and grab my AR-15 with the scope. Just in case I gotta kill a cop today."

Chapter 3

Camille King unlocked the door and stepped inside her big brother's huge suburban house with shopping bags flung over her shoulder. Her best friend, Krystal Hamilton, helped her bring in what she couldn't carry.

"How did Shelton afford this place?" Krystal asked, mesmerized. She looked at the high ceilings and shiny wood mezzanine leading to rooms that she couldn't see from where she stood. There was just as much design on this floor as there was above her. "This is cool, Camille. Man, this is nice."

"Shelton works hard," Camille said, setting the heavy bags on the leather sectional. "So he tries to buy the best."

"I see."

"Thank you for picking me up this morning. I really wanted to get it all done before my brother or Tre Pound got home."

"No problem. Moses told me I could use his car any time I wanted."

"When is he getting out?"

"He doesn't know yet. He just knows there's a confidential informant on his case that's stopping him from getting a good deal. He wanted me to ask you to ask Tre Pound to get him an investigator."

"I'll ask him."

Giddily, Camille started pulling onesies out of all the bags, laying the tiny outfits over the back of the sectional in no particular order. She smiled. She couldn't wait for the next six months to pass.

"Why did you buy all boy clothes?" Krystal asked. "What if it's a girl?"

"It's a boy, I know it. I can feel him inside me."

"Have you told Shelton or Tre Pound yet?"

"Nope."

"Neither one?"

"You know I can't tell them, Krystal."

"Why not? It's not like they can kill your baby daddy. He's already dead."

Camille lied and told Krystal that J-Dub got her pregnant right before Lil' Pat killed him. In reality, she and J-Dub had only gotten a little bit of kissing and 4-play in before Lil' Pat and Hoodey showed up outside his house. It was the perfect lie to tell people. Nobody would be able to disprove it. No one would suspect that Tre Pound was the father.

Krystal sat down on the couch but gave Camille enough room to lay out more clothes. "What are you gonna name him?"

"Levour King, after my cousin."

"After Tre Pound?"

"I like his name," Camille said. "And he's the only one in my family that acts like he loves me. Screw everybody else."

"I wish Dominique was still alive. She would've been too happy for you. I know you remember how bad she wanted a baby."

21

Camille's smile went away at the mention of Dominique, but she kept straightening out onesies.

Off and on, Camille would have nightmares about the day she suffocated Dominique Hayes. She often wondered if she'd still be having the nightmares if she had let Dominique bleed out on her own from the gunshot to her chest. At the time, Camille didn't want to take the chance of her surviving. Her being alive had put a wedge between Camille and Tre Pound, and that just wasn't right or fair. With this baby growing in Camille's belly, she knew that no matter what woman came into Tre Pound's life, he'd make sure she and his baby were loved first.

"Let's not talk about Dominique," said Camille. "She's dead now. Let her rest."

There was a little more than clothes in Camille's bags. She had bottles, bibs, diapers, wipes, everything she could think of. The only problem was hiding all of this stuff from Tre Pound and Shelton until the right time came to tell them she was pregnant.

With the size of this house, she thought, *finding a good hiding spot shouldn't be that hard at all.*

All the purchases were laid out on the leather sectional when they both heard a car pull up in the driveway. Camille raced to the floor-to-ceiling windows and looked out.

"Oh shit!" Camille screamed. "Fuck us!"

"Is it Tre Pound?"

"No, it's the fucking police! Three cars and a damn van!"

Camille shot across the living room to the back of the house. As soon as she unlocked the patio doors to escape out back, SWAT stormed up onto the deck wearing their para-military gear, armed with sub-machine guns. One of them held up four fingers.

"Hold your fire!" the lead balaclava-clad officer shouted to his men. "We have children on the premises!"

Camille locked the doors and ran down the hallway with Krystal close behind.

"I have to get Moses' car," Krystal said in a panic.

"It's blocked in, Krystal. We have to get outta here."

"Why are we running? We didn't do anything wrong."

"Shelly gave me an exit plan in case of emergency," Camille panted, swinging open the basement door. "If the police are here, that means Shelly is in jail. He's my legal guardian so if I get caught, they're gonna stick me in a detention center until God knows when. You will too just for being here. Now get your ass down in this basement!"

The front door boomed as officers battle-rammed it, knocking it so far off the hinges the sturdy door skid into the kitchen. At almost the same time, the glass-encased patio doors on the southside of the house shattered so splendidly that it sprayed thousands of glass bits all over the living room floor.

"Go!" Camille screamed.

The girls marched down the steps into the basement and Camille led the way to the wine cellar.

"The people who owned this house before my brother were doomsday freaks, which is part of the reason why he bought this place," Camille explained to Krystal, opening the cellar doors and getting a cool blast of 30-degree air. "There's a tunnel in here."

Most of the wine slots were filled with nothing less than 50-year-old alcohol. Brugerolle Cognac, Glenavon whisky, including Glenfiddich scotch. Camille tugged hard on the latch welded to the steel door at the back of the cellar. There was a small click followed by a deeper, dungeon-like clank, and then she dragged it open.

"Get inside!" Camille said hurriedly.

They ran down a solid concrete tunnel for about thirty feet, fighting cobwebs the whole way. Then the tunnel opened up into a 120-square-foot bunker fashioned with wood furniture and empty shelves.

"Up here," Camille said, climbing up a rusty red-iron service ladder.

Krystal looked up. "Camille, I'm scared."

Halfway to the top, Camille turned and looked down at the tears in her friend's eyes. "What can you do for Moses if you get arrested? They might not keep you in detention forever, but they'll make you sit. They will, Krystal. Shelly taught me to run."

"I haven't done anything. We're breaking the law if we run."

"Through here!" echoed down the tunnel from one of the officers.

"C'mon, Krystal!"

Krystal shook her head no. "Moses needs me."

"That's why I'm telling you to—" Camille gave up. "Fine."

At the top rung, Camille pushed the hatch open and peeked her head out. She was in her brother's garden, which was extravagantly decorated with vines crawling up-and-through white wood fencing. Camille could see the police roaming through the house.

She hoisted herself up and out, and immediately she heard the police down below ordering Krystal to the ground. Camille saw an escape route. There was a wooded path that broke in between the neighborhood forest, miles of trees that hadn't been torn down by this subdivision. She took off without a second thought.

"Backyard!" yelled an officer.

Sprinting as fast as she could, she looked back and saw a group of about four SWAT men running after her in full tactical gear. She pushed her legs harder, sucking in breaths of air through her nose in a steady rhythm. The tail of her blouse flapped behind her as she flew down the rutted dirt path.

"Get her, Eric! Get her!"

Camille looked back again. There was only one officer chasing her now; the others had tired out, watching and cheering Eric on. He tore off his black mask and propelled himself faster.

Camille was feeling winded now. Her chest burned and she was forced to take big harsh breaths out her mouth. *I'm faster than this,* she said to herself. *This baby in my stomach is slowing me down.* When she saw the end of the path, she got a glimmer of hope. Tre Pound's red Infiniti M was parked on the gravel opening up ahead. She saw him get out the car with an assault rifle.

"C'mere, you little bitch!" she heard behind her.

This fucking cop is so close! Camille panicked. *I'm not gonna make it.*

She saw Tre Pound set the long-barreled rifle on the hood of his car with the weapon's kickstand down. He positioned himself behind the scope. He was aiming at her. He hollered, "If you don't think you can make it, Camille, you better hit the dirt so I can get a good shot!"

Camille pushed her legs faster. She didn't want Tre Pound to have to kill a police officer.

"You better not let that muthafucka catch you!" Tre Pound yelled.

Seneca got out of the car and held the back door open for her. He had a pistol in his hand.

Camille looked behind her again. The cop had dropped back, jogging to a complete stop before bending over and resting his hands on his knees, gasping for breath. Either he had run out of wind or he'd seen the guns Tre Pound and Seneca were holding.

She made it to the car and climbed in the back seat, as Tre Pound and Seneca got back in and slammed their doors shut.

"Why'd you let him get that close up on you?" Tre Pound said angrily. "I know you're faster than that mufucka that was chasing you."

I'm pregnant, asshole!

"I'm sorry," Camille said out loud, trying to catch her breath. "Can we please just get out of here ..."

Chapter 4

The whole King family gathered in Bernice's living room—Tre Pound, Gutta, Seneca, Cash, Camille, and Bernice herself. Sitting on top of the old floor model television, Tre Pound faced his family with hopeful eyes.

"Carlo Masaccio said Shelton should be calling any minute. If he has a bond, he'll be home before the day is over wit'."

Then his cell phone rang.

Tre Pound put it to his ear. "Hello?"

"How's everybody doing?" Shelton asked.

"Good. Everybody's here."

"You got Camille in time?"

"Fa-sho. Piece of cake."

"Okay, put me on speaker phone."

Tre Pound tapped a button on his cell and pointed the speaker toward everyone.

"Listen up everybody," Shelton began. "I shouldn't have to remind yall but this call is recorded. Be careful what you say. That said, I am glad to tell you guys that I've been issued a bond."

Camille let out a girlie "Yippie!" and the rest of the room started clapping.

Tre Pound laughed and asked, "How much is the bond?"

"One million dollars secured," said Shelton.

"That ain't shit," Gutta said excitedly.

Then Shelton spoke again. "But here's the bad news: The Feds froze all my accounts."

Bernice moaned, and so did her boys Cash and Seneca. In one way or another, everyone benefitted from Shelton's income. Bernice didn't have to worry about mortgage because Shelton paid it. Gutta and his wife, Michelle, had their cars paid off by Shelton last year, and Shelton would have paid for Gutta's lawyer if Gutta hadn't wanted to handle his current case on his own. Sometimes Cash, Seneca, and Camille didn't know how good they had it when Shelton would hand them his credit card and tell them to "get what you need." Camille knew it now, though. Tears started running down her cheeks the second her big brother announced his account was frozen. She knew her lifestyle was about to be flipped inside out.

Even Tre Pound benefitted from Shelton's good will. Tre Pound would have never been able to post that half a mill bond two years ago if it weren't for Shelton. Can't forget the brand new Infiniti M he was driving now either. And according to the IRS, Tre Pound was employed by King Financial, which in the past helped him get off probation.

Shelton's voice continued on speaker. "Carlo Masaccio is trying his hardest to get the freeze removed. But that could take months, and I don't want to sit in here that long. In the public's eyes, the longer I sit behind bars, the guiltier I become. So I need everybody to come together to raise this million."

"I have twenty-five hundred dollars saved up," Camille said.

Shelton chuckled. "That's a start. How about you, Tre Pound?"

"I know for a fact I don't have a mill. Total, I can probably get my hands on a quarter of it, maybe even three hundred thousand."

"Anybody else?" Shelton asked.

Gutta brought up his court case and said all his money was tied up in that, but he'd talk to his wife about getting a quick loan from her parents. Between Cash and Seneca, they had ten thousand dollars stashed. And the only money Bernice had in her account was the life insurance check from Cutthroat's death, which she said was almost gone.

"Get all the money yall have together," Shelton told the room, "and whatever amount we have left we'll just have to borrow. I have a few contacts."

After everyone told Shelton they loved him, he hung up. Then everyone started talking at once, trying to figure out how Shelton got caught up and what went wrong. Camille was the most outspoken, the loudest in her belief that, "Somebody is telling' on him! Shelly doesn't make mistakes. Don't let me find out who it is, I swear." Tre Pound was just sitting on the top of the TV by himself thinking of a solution to get Shelton out.

"Okay, listen up," he said all of a sudden. "Like Shelton just said, we gotta pool all our money together. I got a quarter mill, give or take, in a safety deposit box at the bank. But the key is at my house. I need you two"—he aimed two fingers at Seneca and Cash—"to grab that up for me while I head out South and try to gather up a few more ends from a couple friends."

Gutta chuckled. "What friends?"

The whole room knew Tre Pound didn't have any friends anymore. Playa Paul and Stacks were dead, Moses was in federal lockup, and Marlon was trying to kill him. So when he said "friends," he was speaking of drug dealers he could rob for fast lump sums.

"Believe it or not I still got some friends," Tre Pound laughed. "They just don't know they're my friends."

"Why do my sons have to go get that key?" Bernice asked. "Don't the people that's tryna kill you know where you live now? Ain't that why you're staying wit' Shelton? I don't want my boys over there either."

"Aunt Bernice, I can't be everywhere at once," Tre Pound said. "I'm tryna get all this money together as soon as possible."

Gutta put his arm around Bernice and said, "They can handle it, Momma. Me, Shelton, and Tre Pound had a lot more responsibility than that at their age."

"We're good, Momma," said Cash.

"We ain't kids," added Seneca. "I got something' for them 12th Street niggas if they show up. Marlon too. Anybody can get it."

Tre Pound headed out to his car and popped his trunk. He reached in and unfastened the scope from his AR-15. He didn't need the scope anymore; the rest of today's activities would be close range, in-your-face robberies. The type of robberies he was known for. The type of robberies he lived for.

He was slamming the trunk closed when Camille walked up to him. She was wearing hear jean shorts up higher, it seemed—her caramel legs looked longer than they did a few minutes ago—and she had no business coming outside in purple ankle socks.

"What can I do to help?" she asked.

"Just stay in the house and try not to get on Bernice's nerves. It looks like we're gonna be staying here for a little bit. We can't go back to Shelton's house because it's more than likely seized until he gets out. Can you handle that?"

"Yeah. I'm just not staying here by myself. As long as you're here with me, I'm fine being around these people."

"'These people' are your family."

"Did you have a talk with Seneca?" she asked.

"He's not gon' mess wit' you no more."

"What'd you say to him? Did he try to deny it? That muthafuckin' pussy, I hate him."

"Just get in the house, Camille. I got money to get. Tre Block."

Chapter 5

Cash parked his black Chevy Camaro in front of Tre Pound's house on 35th and Agnes. The Camaro was a brawny, supercharged coupe that Shelton bought him for his 17th birthday. He revved the engine to hear it roar again, then he shut the ignition off.

"It still ain't as fast as Tre Pound's Infiniti," said Seneca.

"So what? Get off his dick."

"You should've got an Infiniti. That's what I'ma ask Shelton to get me when my turn comes to get a car."

"Why? Because Tre Pound got one?"

Cash was out the car and slamming his door shut before his little brother could respond. He knew Seneca wanted to be like Tre Pound so bad, and he liked to tease him for it. Cash looked up to Tre Pound too, but since Seneca tried so much to imitate him it made Cash lean more toward Shelton's nature and mannerisms. Cash wanted to be behind a desk someday, just like Shelton, sipping coffee with pointy shoes kicked up on his desk, telling young girls to fetch him more creme and sugar for his cup of decaf—though Cash didn't drink coffee—while talking on the phone to a corporate manager in a foreign language, with two other prime ministers on hold. Shelton let him sit in his desk chair once and it made his mind wander.

Until that time came, though, he'd be in the streets in long-sleeve graphic tees and Air Jordans like he was now, with his little brother lagging behind him. Seneca was always walking slow because he was trying to walk in the same upright stride as Tre Pound.

"Where did you and Tre Pound go today?" Cash asked, as he held the front door open and waited for his little brother to catch up.

"He took me to get my hair cut and teach me how to plot out licks. Because you haven't been taking me wit' you since you got yo new car."

"You don't ever ask to go wit' me."

"That's because you're gone before I wake up."

"Start getting up earlier then."

"No."

"Well that's why you haven't been riding with me."

Cash did feel a little bit guilty. He had been waking up earlier since he got his own car, intentionally leaving Seneca sleep as he made up his bed quietly and got dressed. He didn't want Seneca tagging along with him *all the time* because he had been hooking up with a lot more girls lately—his new car was attracting new pussy. And some of these girls were mature, girls without friends, or girls with friends whom Seneca wouldn't know how to talk to.

"I'll take you with me next time I go out," Cash said.

"I don't wanna go with you no more," Seneca replied.

The house was eerily quiet when they walked in. All the curtains were closed, enshrouding most of the house in darkness, but there was still enough midday light shining in for them to see the condition of the living room. It looked like it had been ransacked—couch pillows tossed on the floor, DVDs scattered about, a single desk drawer sitting in the middle of the hallway that they both had to step over.

"What the fuck happened?" Cash said, astonished.

"I don't know," Seneca uttered, looking around the house in a daze.

"I know you don't know, stupid. It looked like somebody broke in."

The television set was also laying facedown, still plugged up. Seneca tried to pick it up so it would sit upright, but the stand was cracked. He let it fall back down.

"Leave his shit alone," Cash said.

"Tre Pound is gon' be mad as fuck."

"Oh yeah he is. He's gone kill somebody behind this. Let's hurry up and get his deposit key."

They went upstairs, expecting to see more of a mess but everything was in order. Whoever broke in only roughed up the downstairs. Seneca went in the bathroom to take a piss while Cash walked in Tre Pound's room and sat down on his bed, scooting the end table back. There was a small square recess in the sheetrock that he could barely pull loose. He had to stick his fingernails in the side cuts and pry it out. The deposit key sat in the hole, which he put in his pocket.

"Both of yall bitch-ass muthafuckas get on the fuckin' floor!"

Cash looked up and saw his brother being pushed inside the room. Marlon was standing in the doorway with an AR-15 equipped with a set of ammunition drums. He looked more rugged and beaten down. His light skin was even lighter from what looked like lack of sun, and he had a full beard—they had never seen Marlon without a fresh haircut. He looked like a woodsman.

Marlon jerked the assault rifle at them in a gesture for them to move now. They sat down on the floor against the bed.

"Now where the fuck is Tre Pound?" Marlon asked, squatting down so he was eye level with them. "If yall give me his life, on my dead sister I will spare yours."

Chapter 6

Gutta had his seat belt on. It sat tight against his broad chest, as he drove and watched the road ahead. No radio. Just him and his thoughts. He had just looked up and saw a highway sign that told him he was halfway home. It surprised him. He was so in a daze he hadn't realized how many miles he'd driven.

He thought he would feel good, feel free now that he'd completed his obligation as an informant. He gave the FBI their big prize—his older cousin Shelton King. And before that he gave them Moses, and before that he gave them Tommy and Tony, and before that he cooperated with the FBI and the ATF in apprehending Marlon Hayes and securing a stockpile of military weapons.

And before that ...

How many people had he helped send to jail?

He'd lost count.

It was eating him up now, gnawing at his conscience. Now that it was all over, he wondered if he shouldn't have cooperated, wondered if he should have just snatched a prison sentence and did his time. He probably would have been released by now, and instead of driving home in this Dodge Dart with a too-tight seat belt, he could have been standing in the center of a welcome-home party, two corkless champagne bottles clutched in both fists, expensive froth pouring down his knuckles as his family cheered his name, a name he once earned.

Gutta, hooray! Gutta, hooray!

He could have been proud of himself.

His head hit the back of the seat and he gritted his teeth hopelessly, but he still had his eyes on the road. Deep down he wanted to snatch the wheel left and slam into oncoming traffic. *I don't deserve to live,* he thought. *I sold my own family out for freedom I didn't even take advantage of. I let my freedom go to waste. I've done nothing with my life but take from others. What do I have to show for myself that has made cooperating with the police worth it? Nothing, Gutta. You have nothing!*

He unclipped his phone from his belt and called his wife.

"Hello?"

"Michelle, I can't take it," Gutta said in desperation. "I can't live with this shit on my chest."

"What are you talking' about, baby? Where are you?"

"I'm on my way there. I just came from the family meeting and Shelton spoke to all of us over the phone. I felt like shit the whole time he was talking. I put him there!"

"Calm down, Maurice. We talked about this. Shelton is a fighter. He'll get out of there. He has the best legal team."

"What if he finds out I sent his files to the FBI?"

"He won't! As long as you support him in getting released he'll never suspect a thing. It's over now. You no longer have to be an informant. You did what you had to do to avoid prison so we could be together. Now we can do what we talked about."

When Gutta was first approached by prosecution with the confidential informant deal, he and Michelle talked it over. She told him she wasn't sure if she'd be able to stay with him if he had to do a long prison sentence. She wanted a family, kids, she wanted a ring. So he took the deal. But after Gutta's first time wearing a wire, he decided he didn't want to bring kids into this world while he was a snitch. It would be too unsafe for them. So he and Michelle agreed that as soon as his legal obligation to the State of Missouri was met, they'd try to have their first child.

"Maurice, make love to me," Michelle said through the phone. "Come home and make love to me and you'll feel so much better, I promise."

"I wanna kill myself," Gutta told her.

"Don't talk like that. That's not the man I married. I married a man who loves me and his family. It doesn't matter what you did to Shelton. You still love him."

"We need to talk to your parents. See if we can put together some money for his bond."

"Okay. Whatever we have to do. Just come home and make love—"

Michelle suddenly screamed in terror, and her screams faded into the background from being yanked away from the phone. Gutta heard a man telling his wife to quit hollering, threatening to shoot her.

"Michelle!" Gutta yelled into the phone. "Michelle! Micheeeeeelle!"

She couldn't hear him. Whoever was man-handling her asked for Tre Pound.

Gutta threw his phone down and stomped on the gas pedal. He clicked off his seatbelt and sat up on the wheel as he swerved through an intersection, screeching into a turn that almost sent him spinning out of control but the back end righted itself. He was almost home. And he didn't know what he was going to do once he got there. How many people were there? He didn't have a gun. Part of his informant deal had stipulated no weapons unless on assignment.

I don't need a gun, Gutta thought. He once choked two men unconscious at the same time, a throat in each hand, squeezed until the first one passed out and the second one pissed himself. The old Gutta would make due.

He drove up on the curb into his front lawn, leaving a dirty tire path gorged in his grass. As he jumped out he barely noticed the three cars parked along the curb. A Grand National, a Suburban, another Buick sedan.

He was too focused on saving his wife.

He left his driver's door open and leaped up onto his porch and barged through his front door into a room full of men, seven total. But Gutta had no fear—he tackled the first one he saw.

Punched him hard, drew blood instantly.

Someone near Michelle yelled, "Get that muthafucka! Who was supposed to be watching the door?! Get his ass!"

Gutta punched him again, though the goon was out with the first blow. A couple of the men grabbed onto him, the bigger of the two wrapping Gutta up in a headlock. Gutta was wheezing now from lack of air, but had the strength to throw an elbow and connect with ribs. The guy behind Gutta *oomphed* up a gust of breath, and with the second elbow he let Gutta go.

Gutta swung around and grabbed the guy by the neck of his shirt, scrunched it in his fists and yanked tight and head-butted him viciously.

Blood poured down his mouth quick and natural, and Gutta didn't realize he was holding him up until he let go. The brawny guy's body hit the floor in folds, knees first, then sitting on his heels and folding forward in mock prayer. He was out.

"Bitch nigga!"

Gutta heard the curse but didn't see the pistol until it came across his face. He stumbled into someone who grabbed him firmly, and for a split second Gutta thought it was a friend holding him up, until a pistol bashed across his face again.

He collapsed. Gravity had his head glued to the floor. He felt liquidy, and his strength had dissolved.

Then he heard their voices.

"This mufucka came in like a bull."

"Who is he?

"That's Tre Pound."

"No it's not. Who is it, Spook?"

"That's Gutta, Tre Pound's cousin."

Gutta's vision was a fog, as he struggled to gaze across the floorboards at Michelle, who was wiggling around on the floor, restrained by her hair. The bald, dark-skinned man who Gutta knew by the name Spook had his wife's micro braids twisted in his fist as she screamed and tugged and squirmed around as if she was sitting on ice, screaming more with each yank to get free but Spook's grip was anchored in her scalp. She was his slave.

"Michelle ..." whispered Gutta.

Then a boot came down on his face.

***

"Is this it?" Tre Pound asked everyone in the living room as he peeked inside the duffel bag hanging from his shoulder. "What's this, thirty racks? Yall gotta be kidding' me. All that hustling' and all yall came up wit' is thirty?"

He pushed the money around the bag's inner non-stretch coated nylon, searching for the larger denomination bills that weren't there.

"What the fuck am I supposed to do with this? I can't bond my cousin outta jail with this."

"That's all we got, damn man."

It was one of the older teens that spoke, a thin but muscular young brotha named Mike Folk with tattoos covering his forearms. Tre Pound knew this was Mike's dope house. Of the seven teenagers laying on the ground, he was the only one that dared to look up at Tre Pound.

"It's hella other niggas in Kansas City that's getting' way more money than us that you could've robbed," said Mike Folk, then he pointed to the rear of the house. "The niggas on the other side of Prospect is checkin' way more than us."

Tre Pound aimed the M-16 a quarter-inch down from Mike Folk's head. He didn't aim dead-on because the weapon's kickback would jerk up when he squeezed the trigger. "I just came from visiting them niggas on the other side of Prospect," Tre Pound said. "After I took their stash they told me to come over here, said yall was doing numbers like them too. So I thought I'd stop by."

"Why the fuck are you stealing from us, my nigga? We fuck wit' niggas from the Tre."

"As you should. But this isn't about 'hoods. This is about dues. My uncle Cutthroat laid the groundwork for

41

you little niggas to hustle. My big cousin Shelton opened doors that brought in dope from coasts all over the country, brought in dope from bosses who knew nothing' about Kansas City until he—"

"Who fuckin' cares?" another boy said, looking up. "You're not a hustler. Just get the fuck on outta here."

Then another teen to Tre Pound's left spoke up with a smart remark too. Tre Pound actually had to take his eyes off of Mike Folk to see who said it. This was insubordination. Cutthroat told him there would be times when drug dealers didn't cooperate. Men in groups, especially young men, often grew bold and courageous, even suicidal. *Always control the situation,* Cutthroat had said. *Never let it get out of hand.*

When Tre Pound saw one the boys try to stand up, he switched weapons—he let the M-16 hang against his side from its shoulder strap and quickly pulled his Glock 9 pistol from his waist. The young boy who had moved was on his feet now and starting to say something about Tre Pound not being a real gangsta when Tre squeezed the trigger.

Shot him low, in the leg.

He fell on a friend, screaming.

"Let another one of you muthafuckas get up, I'm using the M-16!" roared Tre Pound. "And if I kill one, I'm killing' all!"

"You got all our cash," Mike Folk said hurriedly. He was looking down at the floor now. "That's it, I swear, my nigga."

"I want all of you pussies to take yall jewelry off! Right now, take it off! Yall done pissed me off!"

There were only a few of them who had jewelry on, even less who had pieces actually worth something. Tre

Pound's phone started ringing. He set his duffle bag down and took it out, saw Cash's number on the screen. He answered it.

"I'm in the middle of getting money right now, Cash. I can't talk. Did yall find the key?"

"They found it. But I got it now."

Tre Pound froze at hearing Marlon's voice. His pulse started beating faster. *I shouldn't have sent Cash and Seneca,* he thought as his mind raced. *I should've went myself.*

"Where's my cousins at?" Tre Pound asked.

"They're here," Marlon said. "They're still alive, for now."

"Let me talk to one of 'em."

Marlon must have faced the phone at his cousins because he heard them both speak at the same time: "He took the key and he—" "Tre, he's by himself but he caught us slippin'—" "—got us sitting here with a chop in our face—" "and he took our straps—"

Then their voices were gone as Marlon put the phone back up to his ear. "Ya hear that?"

"I'm through playing' wit' you," said Tre Pound. "Next time I see you, I'm takin' yo face off."

"You can see me now, muthafucka! I'm at yo house right now! I don't wanna kill yo cousins but I will. If you come, I'll let 'em live. Maybe."

"If you're there when I get there, you already know what's gon' happen."

"I do. I'ma gun yo ass down. You know my aim is sharp, that's why you running from me."

"I don't run, pussy-ass nigga. You've been knowing me long enough to know that."

"Yeah, I know how you move. You move like a bitch. You prey on the weak niggas in the streets. You move shady and sneaky. Fuckin' yo homeboy's little sister, getting' her killed. You set yo own friends up to get killed."

"Nigga, don't put that on me. You killed Stacks and Playa Paul. Those were yo bullets. That's yo fucked-up ass that did that, all because I stuck my dick in yo little sister. I didn't kill Dominique. You know who killed her, nigga."

"If it wasn't for you, she'd still be alive."

"Keep telling' yo'self that. But it was my little cousin Camille that killed that nigga Young Ray for killing Dominique. You should be thanking' me and my family, but you're over there witta gun in my people's face. It ain't no making' up for that, Marlon. I'm on yo head now."

"There you go runnin' yo mouth again. Shut the fuck up and bring yo ass on."

"I'll be there. Tre block."

Tre Pound was looking at all the drug dealers laying on the ground, as he thought about how to get the best drop on Marlon. One thing Marlon was good at was shooting guns. His father, once a military veteran, taught him how to hold, aim and field strip everything from a simple 9mm handgun to an M1 Carbine down to the buttplate screw. And along with skill, Marlon had the advantage being inside the house.

Tre Pound needed to even the odds. His uncle Cutthroat told him there was always a way to gain ground on an enemy. *Use all the resources you have available,* Cutthroat had said. *Nothing is off limits if you win. But if you lose, no matter by what means, you'll always be known as the lesser man.*

"None of you muthafuckas better move," Tre Pound said to the room, as he turned and walked into the hallway. He could still see just about all the dealers laying on the ground from where he stood, even the one moaning with a bullet in his leg.

So he picked up his phone and dialed a number he thought he would never have to dial in his lifetime.

After a couple rings, someone picked up.

"911, what's your emergency?"

"I'd like to report a break-in," Tre Pound said. "I think someone broke into my house."

Chapter 7

"Tre Pound is gonna show up wit' all his niggas," Seneca said to Marlon in a threatening voice. "You really think he's gonna let you walk out of his house alive? You got life fucked up."

"Seneca, be quiet," Cash said.

Marlon was re-checking his rifle. He detached his clip, checked the rounds, then popped it back in. "It's a better chance yall won't make it outta here alive," he said to them.

Cash watched him methodically inspect the rest of the weapon. Marlon peered down the barrel, wiped the rim of it with his shirt. Cash knew that Tre Pound had guns stashed all around his house and wondered if he could get to one fast enough without being shot. Tre Pound kept a pistol tucked in between the mattress they were sitting against. Or had Marlon already found them all?

"Tre Pound doesn't have any homeboys anyway," Marlon said. "The niggas he did have, he crossed. Two of 'em are dead and the other one is locked up. I was his last homie on the streets. Don't nobody else fuck wit' yo cousin. He's too scandalous."

"If he calls my big brother Gutta, that's yo ass," said Seneca. "They gon' come and tear you apart."

"Gutta ain't coming' over here. Niggas already got him hemmed up." Marlon seen the surprise on their faces and continued without a blink. "Yeah, Gutta might already be dead. I told Spook and his niggas where he lived, just in case Tre Pound was hiding over there. But knowing Tre Pound, he probably was hiding out over Shelton's because he knows I don't know where he lives. Matter-of-fact, let me see what's going on over Gutta's house."

Marlon leaned against the wall with a knee bent, then made his call. He put it on speaker phone so Cash and Seneca could listen in.

"Hello?"

"Spook, this is Marlon. I got Tre Pound's little cousins here in front of my rifle and I just got off the phone wit' Tre Pound. He's on his way here."

"So what's the play?" Spook asked.

"Well, his little cousins just told me he might try and contact Gutta."

Cash elbowed Seneca hard in the side for giving up that information.

Through the speaker phone, Spook's voice said, "This nigga Gutta ain't takin' any calls right now. He just woke up and his jaw is swollen."

"Okay. But you know Tre Pound; he'll always try to do some underhanded shit to come out on top. Be on the lookout for him. He might try and stop through there before he comes here."

"I hope he does."

Marlon hung up and put the phone in his pocket. He looked at all the items on the night stand that he confiscated from Cash and Seneca. He scooted their guns to the side and picked up the safety deposit box key and twirled it around in his fingers, as if he couldn't wait for the owner to come claim it.

Seneca said, "You won't be able to use that key at the bank. They'll have you on camera."

"I don't want his money," Marlon said. "I just want his life."

Cash was staring. Couldn't stop staring at Marlon, a person he had looked up to at one point, a person Tre Pound had once spoken highly of, a person Shelton even said, "has the right attitude and love for his kind to survive forever in the streets." The love looked gone, Cash thought. How did Marlon go from being a loyal homeboy to an enemy almost overnight? It was mind-boggling.

Marlon caught him staring. He gave Cash a look: *You got something to say to me?*

Yes, Cash did.

"Tre Pound didn't kill Dominique."

Marlon fired back, "That's none of yo business, lil' nigga. I like yall, that's why I haven't killed yall yet. I still kinda look at yall as my little brothers. But don't speak on shit yall know nothing' about."

"He didn't fuckin' kill her," Seneca blurted with a toughness that a hostage shouldn't have had. "Tre Pound told us you're mad that she died and you're taking it out on him. What kind of nigga are you? You used to be a real nigga. Now you a ho."

As much as Cash wanted his little brother to shut the hell up, he had said what Cash was thinking, in so many words. Marlon was noticeably mad. Madder than before. He was still leaning against the wall, but he was holding the assault rifle with two hands now—it wasn't pointed at them, yet—and he was clutching it so tight Cash thought he heard the rubber on the forward grip crinkle. He was furious, but trying to hold it in.

"Let me tell yall something about Tre Pound," Marlon said. "He's poison. I tried to overlook it when Stacks first introduced me to him. I heard about how greasy he was to niggas in the streets who were stand-up guys. But he had never did me wrong so I didn't really care. Even when all his foulness started to affect me—getting into fights wit' niggas I didn't know, niggas approaching my little sister for information, one of my cars getting shot up—I still fucked wit' Tre Pound because he was my nigga."

"That comes wit' the dope life," Seneca stated. It sounded like something Tre Pound told him.

"No, that comes wit' being associated wit' Tre Pound," Marlon replied. "Yall will never know how easy it is to move unseen in the town because he's yall's cousin. But there's ways to get money in the streets without all the drama. With Tre Pound, it's everyday nonsense. But like I said, he became my nigga because, even though he was greasy, he was smart and I liked picking his brain. I never thought he would play me like he did everybody else. It was more than him fucking my little sister. It was him doing it behind my back. Sneaky shit you don't do to yo homeboy. It made me wonder if he became cool with me and hung out at my crib just to get close to her. He used me. He used Stacks. He used Playa Paul. He used Moses. He used all of us for protection, to make other niggas think he had an army. We were his pawns. He'll use yall too. He has no love for nobody but himself and his own reputation."

Cash remembered something Shelton said to him about Tre Pound a few weeks ago. Shelton told him to "learn from Tre Pound, but be your own man." Thinking about it now after hearing what Marlon just let out, Cash wondered if Shelton had been warning him. Warning him to *not* be like Tre Pound. Learn how *not* to move in the streets. Now that Cash was really letting the thoughts roll around in his head, he was pretty sure that Shelton had spoken more highly of Marlon over the years than he had Tre Pound.

There was a knock at the front door and it startled everyone. Marlon picked their guns up off the nightstand and stuffed them in his pockets; the handles bulged out each side of his jacket. He put the key in his back pocket, then ordered them to go downstairs. Cash tried to take his time standing up, hoping Marlon would turn his head long enough for him to slip his hand in between the mattress and feel for one of Tre Pound's hidden guns—if a gun was still there—but Marlon's eyes stayed fixed on them.

"Move!" Marlon barked. "Get yall asses downstairs now!"

Cash and Seneca started walking, and Marlon even pushed Cash in the back with the barrel to hurry him up. The whole way down the steps, up until they were standing in front of the front door, Marlon prodded Cash with the barrel.

Marlon poked him again and said, "Look out the window and tell me who you see."

Cash pulled the curtains back and looked out. There were two police officers standing on the front porch. One saw him, a Black officer who put his hand on his holstered weapon and pointed to the front door for him to open it. He yelled for him to open it, and Marlon heard.

"Who the fuck is it?" Marlon said impatiently. "That didn't sound like Tre Pound."

"It's the police," said Cash. He was surprised to see them himself.

"Bullshit ..." Marlon peeked out and saw the cops. They saw him too and started banging on the front door. "That bitch-ass nigga Tre Pound called the police?!"

"KCPD, open up. We got a call about a break-in."

"Fuckin' coward!" Marlon cursed.

"We know you're in there. Open up, fellas!"

Cash kept staring at Marlon, waiting for an opportunity. Tre Pound always kept one of his biggest weapons in the hall closet, which Cash had just rested his back against quietly, as Marlon cocked his assault rifle and aimed it at the front door. Cash thought, *I hope it's still in here,* as he pulled his arm behind his back to secretly grab the knob. He looked at Seneca and gave him a wide-eyed look, a "distract him" type of look, but Seneca's eyebrows scrunched in confusion. Cash mouthed the words, "get his attention," and pointed at Marlon and it seemed like his little brother finally understood.

"Do you want me to tell them to leave?" Seneca asked Marlon.

Marlon looked at him as if he was stupid, and it gave Cash just enough time without being fully seen to turn the knob. No squeak. He bent his arm inside the closet, painfully, and he felt the tip of a muzzle against his fingertips.

"If you open that door they're gonna barge in here," Marlon said.

The cops banged harder. "Open this door, goddammit!" one of them yelled. "Yall are going to jail whether you like it or not. If I was yall, I would've at least broke into a house in a better neighborhood."

The other officer laughed.

Marlon's jaws were clenched. "Tre Pound thinks I'ma

run," he said, more to himself. "He thinks he can outsmart me. He thinks he won."

Marlon suddenly opened fire, sent bullets flying through the front door. Rapid, thunderous bursts. Seneca ducked for cover by the stairs, as Marlon waved the assault rifle in a sweeping motion to catch the whole area of the front porch where the cops were standing.

That's when Cash yanked the assault rifle out of the closet; it was an AK-47 that Tre Pound let him shoot three or four times when he first purchased it. Cash chambered a bullet—*click-clack!*—and Marlon heard it and swung around as Cash lifted it up.

Cash fired first.

It was a quick, uncontrolled nervous reaction. He missed in his barrage of shots, but was close enough to make Marlon stumble to the side and dive into the kitchen.

Cash sprayed bullets into the kitchen too.

And when Marlon returned fire, Cash was already running to the back of the house where he saw Seneca go. He spotted Seneca hiding behind a love seat with a handgun he probably found under the cushion.

"Go get the car," Seneca said to him. "I got Marlon."

"No you don't, fool." Cash grabbed him by his arm. "C'mon, Seneca!"

The brothers went out the back door. They ran around the house to the front, and when Cash stopped abruptly, Seneca bumped into him.

"What is it?" Seneca asked.

One of the cops was kneeling down on the front porch with his hand on his dead partner's chest. He had his radio in his other hand. "Officer down! 35th and Agnes, officer down!"

Bleeding himself, the officer stormed into the house with his pistol drawn.

"C'mon," Cash said.

He and Seneca ran over to the Camaro and got in. Cash started it up and skirted away from the curb and down away from the house. He was sure he heard more gunfire start up again from inside, from Marlon unloading more ammunition, maybe from the cop too firing back.

Cash kept driving, speeding, didn't look back.

***

Gutta just wanted to sit next to his wife. He hated that she was so far away, laying against the couch on the floor, crying softly. Spook was sitting on the couch with his black boot propped up on her arm like she was his ottoman. Michelle gazed at Gutta, whimpering, with pleading eyes that screamed, *Do something, Gutta! Help me!*

"Will you tell yo wife to shut the fuck up, please?" Spook said, scratching his own shiny dark bald head with the rounded hammer-end of his firearm. "I'm about two seconds away from shooting this ho. I can't take these whimpers."

Gutta was seething. But there wasn't much he could do. There was a guy in a black tee and gloves pointing an assault rifle down at him as he sat weak on the floor. One squeeze and the bullet would force a path through the top of his head and splash out his temple. There were two more with guns standing around impatiently, bored, one of them thumbing his smartphone. The other two guys Gutta had knocked out earlier had been taken home by the strong guy who had grabbed ahold of Gutta from behind. That took the count down from seven niggas to four.

The black tee goon nudged Gutta with his rifle. "My nigga Spook just asked you a question. Get'cho wife under control, playa. That crying shit is irritating."

Gutta cut his eyes, seeing how close the muzzle was to his face. He could grab it, twist it, and even if this guy managed to pull the trigger his aim would be deflected. The worst that would happen was Gutta's ear drums might explode, and grabbing the muzzle would sear his palm. It would be worth the risk ... if Spook wasn't so close to his wife. Spook could shoot her dead like a dog, stand up and start firing at Gutta before Gutta could effectively yank away the assault rifle.

It was too risky. Unless Gutta could get Spook away from her somehow ...

"Michelle, I'ma get us outta this, okay?" Gutta tried to sound soothing, but with his voice heavy from fatigue and pain, he knew he wasn't convincing her. "They want Tre Pound, they don't want us."

"True," Spook said. "And as soon as I get the call that Tre Pound is dead, I'll let yall go."

Gutta didn't believe him.

"Please let us go," Michelle whined.

"Michelle, don't beg!" Gutta snapped. He tried to sit up. And the guy standing over him with the rifle touched the muzzle against the side of his head, against his skin. A warning not to try anything. Gutta didn't care. He said to Spook, "I know why you want Tre Pound. You think he killed yo homeboys Row and Drought Man."

"I don't think, I know," Spook said.

"You know *wrong*. Especially wit' Drought Man. If Tre Pound killed him, he would've got found guilty at trial."

"The judicial system got it wrong, not me," Spook countered. "He just had a good lawyer, that muthafuckin'

Carlo Masaccio. But we all know Tre Pound did that shit. I don't need the court to tell me he did it. Shit, I'm glad they found him not guilty. He doesn't deserve prison."

"I'm telling you facts, Spook. Tre Pound just got the blame, but he didn't kill Row and Drought Man. I know who did, though."

Spook leaned forward to get a better look at Gutta. In that little bit of movement his weight shifted, so his boot was now pressing down harder on Michelle's arm. She howled with her palm over her mouth. "Tre Pound is still gon' die, but I'll entertain you for a second. Who killed my niggas?"

"It's not about being entertained. This is the truth. Real shit."

"Who killed 'em then?"

Gutta had thought Tre Pound murdered Drought Man too at one point. It wasn't until Tre Pound made bond on Drought Man's murder and Gutta invited him over for drinks and Kush to celebrate, that he found out the truth. Gutta called him stupid for leaving his fingerprints on a shell casing, and that's when Tre Pound told him he didn't do it. *Yo brother Shelton did that shit,* Tre Pound had said, as he poured himself another vodka-wine mix. *But it's still my fault for not cleaning the rounds prior to giving Shelton the AK-47. Fuck it, I'll take the fall.* A couple weeks ago Tre Pound even told Gutta that Shelton killed Row outside of a hospital.

Gutta could always count on Tre Pound to give him information. Tre Pound told him about Marlon's interstate gun ring and Moses' cocaine plug, among other things. Gutta turned lots of secondhand info over to his assigned law enforcement agent, regrettably, because he got nothing but a pat on the back and sometimes a small stipend—the amount varied depending on the severity of the crime and the likelihood of a conviction. Gutta hated using Tre Pound; it was against everything he was taught (one of his father's main mantras was *never swindle family*), but Gutta had to assist in so many arrests per quarter to stay out of prison.

"Who killed my niggas?" Spook asked again.

Gutta wasn't going to let the truth roll off his tongue this time. His informant days were done. So he said, "*I* killed those niggas. They were in the way."

Spook immediately hopped to his feet and stormed over to Gutta. He pointed his pistol down at Gutta's head. Two firearm's in Gutta's face now.

"You think I'ma let you say that shit?!" Spook spat. "I was gon' let you live. But you wanna disrespect the dead by lying? Is that what you wanna do?"

"I'm not lying," Gutta said, staring at the weapons, working himself up to try and take them from these men. One mistake and he was dead.

"Yes, you are, muthafucka. You just tryna protect yo bitch-ass cousin." Spook clicked the hammer back. "Tell me the fuckin' truth!"

"The truth is he didn't do it!" Michelle screamed. "It wasn't my husband. It wasn't Tre Pound. It was Shelton!"

That revelation caused everyone to look at her, to see the despair in her eyes and the thinness of her skin that made her bony body look like it had taken enough suffering. Gutta wished he wouldn't have told her who really killed Drought Man and Row. But there wasn't much he could do now. He had to take advantage of the distraction.

"Say that again," Spook said to her.

"It wasn't Maurice. It was Shelton King. He used Tre Pound's gun to kill Drought Man so his business—"

Michelle screamed when she saw Gutta grab onto both weapons pointed in his face. The assault rifle went off, Gutta wasn't hit but the explosion deafened him, so he snatched the pistol away from Spook and jumped to his feet. He was too close to raise the gun for a kill shot in time—every millisecond counted at this point—so he threw a quick elbow that broke the nose of the black-tee-wearing goon. The goon went down, with Gutta still fisting the barrel of the assault rifle and the goon still holding the rifle's shoulder strap at the other end. Gutta shot him with the pistol so he'd let go.

He had both weapons now.

He aimed and fired the pistol at the other two goons. The one with the smartphone went down first, the other was pushed through the window by the impact of the bullet.

Gutta looked around for Spook.

He was gone.

"He ran out the front!" Michelle screamed.

In a couple quick strides Gutta was at the window where the goon he shot was laying haphazardly on the windowsill in shattered glass, half of his body in, other half hanging outside. Gutta yanked him into the house and threw his body on the floor so he could peer outside.

He saw Spook getting inside the black Grand National. Spook was pulling off as Gutta positioned the assault rifle on the windowsill.

Gutta pulled the trigger and the power of the assault rifle jerked his whole body. He held the trigger down and the automatic fire continued until the Grand National was no longer in sight. Gutta hoped he hit the car, at least.

"Maurice, help me!"

He turned to his wife, ran to her. Her arm was bleeding badly. So much blood for such a skinny woman.

"It feels numb," she cried.

Gutta picked her up and carried her out of the house.

Chapter 8

For the first half hour after Michelle got her arm stitched up, it was all about the nurses. It seemed like every nurse from every floor was in and out the room, chatting with Michelle, making her laugh, and teasing her about being a patient. "You still gotta come to work tomorrow," one said, and they all laughed. At one point there were six nurses in the room at once, six girls in scrubs that were all trying to talk at the same time.

When they left, it was just the family. Gutta, who was sitting on the hospital bed with Michelle, brushed his fingers through her hair gently. Bernice, Cash, Seneca, Tre Pound and Camille were present too. Tre Pound was one of the first ones here after Gutta called him, so he had a comfy chair seat. Camille was sitting on his lap.

Before the nurses started showing up Tre Pound had gotten a quick run-down on what happened at Gutta's house and his own house on 35th Street. Tre Pound was mad that Michelle got shot. Not because he cared about her, but because of the principle of Spook touching someone in his family and the fact that Spook felt like he could get away with it. That was what burned Tre Pound. But he was even angrier that Marlon had his deposit key. He needed that money in the deposit box to help free Shelton, who would be calling any minute.

Gutta said to Tre Pound, "They would've killed us both if I didn't do something. We're blessed that Michelle only caught one in the arm."

Tre Pound didn't get a chance to respond because Cash spoke up.

"That's the same situation me and Seneca was in. I knew I had to get my hands on one of yo guns, Tre Pound. I knew you had some hid around the house. If I wouldn't have grabbed one, Marlon would've smoked our ass."

"I helped too," Seneca said.

"I didn't say you didn't."

Gutta said, "I took out four of them 12th Street niggas. Or six. It was six. They had to carry out two that I knocked out when I first got there." Gutta laughed. "I killed four of 'em though. Gangsta shit, cousin!"

Tre Pound was sort of listening to them. It sounded like his cousins were competing for his attention or approval. Tre Pound was more concerned with Camille. Her booty resting on his thigh, her arm around his neck, the closeness giving him a strong whiff of her body scent. A shower smell. It reminded him of when he opened his bedroom door and she was standing there in just a bath robe. *Do you have any bodywash, Tre Pound? I don't use soap.* He remembered her flashing her breasts, him pushing her down violently, how beautiful she looked laying on the floor crying.

It was arousing him now. His groin pulsed.

He knew Camille felt it but she didn't move. She was acting as if she sat in his lap every day, acting normal, listening and laughing as Cash and Seneca argued over who had been more scared.

Tre Pound wanted her to move.

"You were super scared," Cash said to his little brother. "I found you hiding behind the sofa."

"I wasn't hiding," Seneca growled. "I was taking cover. Stop tryna embarrass me."

Gutta said, "What do you think the police will do to me, Tre Pound? I got three bodies in my house. Should I call 'em? That's self-defense, right?"

"Somebody called the police over to yo house too, Tre Pound," said Cash. "Marlon was saying you called 'em. You didn't call 'em, did you?"

Seneca got mad. "I told you already he didn't call 'em. Why would you ask him that, stupid? That was the neighbors that called the police, right Tre Pound?"

"I called the police," Tre Pound revealed.

It stunned everyone. Even Bernice's hand paused inside her Chex Mix bag as she raised an eyebrow. Camille took her arm from around his neck and looked at him side-eyed.

"You did what?" Camille asked.

"I called the police," Tre Pound said again, clearly. "Cutthroat always taught me to use every resource available at my disposal. The police are pawns; they're here to serve us. If there's no other recourse, you gotta do what you gotta do. Don't be scared to use the police. They use us."

Gutta took that as his cue to call in the bodies in his house. He stood up and walked over to the other side of the room, putting his phone up to his ear. Camille wrapped her arm back around Tre Pound's neck, as if she accepted his explanation. She seemed to be laying closer into him now.

Just as much as he wanted her to sit somewhere else, there was this strange feeling inside him beckoning her, a sensation that was feeding feverishly off her warmth and energy. Something inside of him wanted more of her badly.

And he hated it.

His phone rang.

"Move," Tre Pound said to Camille. "Get up so I can get my phone."

She rose up, but her hand was still on the back of his seat as if she was going to sit right back down in his lap after he got his phone out. It made him wonder if her body had suddenly gone into withdrawal too. Tre Pound pulled his phone out of his pocket and saw that it was Shelton calling. He put it on speakerphone.

"Wussup, my nigga?" Tre Pound said.

Camille sat back down. Tre Pound let her.

Shelton's voice came through, hopeful: "So how much money did we get together?"

"We're short," Tre Pound said.

"How short?"

"All we have is a quarter million. I pulled in some cash from a couple friends, but the trip to the deposit box got intercepted by Marlon."

Gutta had just gotten off the phone with the police. He put his phone in his pocket and said to Shelton, "We're at the hospital right now, bro. It was a hit put down by Marlon and Spook. They teamed up. Marlon ambushed Seneca and Cash at Tre Pound's crib, and Spook and his 12th Street niggas ambushed me and Michelle at my house. They tried to kill us, bro. But I got us out of there. Michelle got shot though."

"How are Cash and Seneca doing?" Shelton asked.

Cash and Seneca said they were fine.

"They did good," said Gutta. "They shot their way

out of there just like I did. True Kings, if I must say so myself."

"Okay, we gotta get the rest of that bond money," Shelton said urgently. "I asked a favor from Hoodey. He said give him 48 hours if we needed the full million. But since yall got together a quarter of it, maybe Gutta can come up with the rest in a shorter time frame. Tre Pound, I need you to call him after I hang up to see if yall can set something up for tomorrow."

"Fuck that nigga," Tre Pound said adamantly. "We don't need any money from Hoodey's ass. Kings don't borrow."

"He's our only option right now."

"I can get the rest of the money on my own. Just give me a few more days. I'll make the streets pay up."

"You can't keep milking the streets, my nigga. If you press too hard, they'll start pressing back. You got enough niggas on yo heels."

"Hoodey is a lame," Tre Pound stated. "I know you didn't forget how he sent his little brother Lil' Pat to a house where Camille was. Hoodey hyped Pat up to kill the nigga Camille was with. Camille could've got hurt or killed. Fuck that nigga Hoodey."

"I never felt like I was in danger," Camille said.

"Camille, shut up," Tre Pound countered.

Bernice chimed in. She was chewing on pretzels as she spoke. "Tre Pound, don't disobey yo big cousin. Just call the Hoodey man he's talking about and get it over with."

Gutta agreed to make the call. "I'll do it," he said to Shelton. "I'll call him first thing in the morning. Maybe we can have you out by tomorrow evening."

Shelton thanked everyone for trying to help out and wished Michelle a speedy recovery. He was still on the phone when Tre Pound shoved Camille off his lap and stormed out the room. He was waiting on an elevator, thinking of maybe telling Shelton he would call Hoodey— and then just rob him and kill him after he got the money.

Camille came over and wrapped an arm around his at the elbow. He pulled away.

"I know how you're feeling," she said. "I don't like borrowing shit from people either."

"Go back in there and sit down before somebody takes yo seat."

"I told Cash he could sit there. Where are you going?"

"None of yo business."

"Are you staying at Bernice's house tonight?"

"Yeah. Where else am I going to sleep at, Camille? Shelton's house got seized. Two cops got killed at my house, three or four niggas got smoked at Gutta's. Where else I'ma go?"

"One of yo bitch's houses."

There was that jealousness in her voice again.

The elevator doors opened up. Tre Pound stepped on and kept tapping the "close doors" button so he wouldn't have to see Camille's sexy smirk.

"Bye," she smiled.

"Tre block," he said as the doors slid together.

Chapter 9

"So who's Camille?"

Buttercup asked the question as she was rolling over onto her stomach—from missionary to doggystyle. Tre Pound flopped his dick on top of her lower back, at the start of her ass crack, and dry-humped her from behind to get some friction going against his undershaft, get some blood flowing through him. He was having a difficult time getting erect.

"What'd you say to me?" Tre Pound asked.

"I asked you who Camille is. You called me her name three times already."

"I don't know any Camille. My bad, homey."

"That's a lie. You have a cousin named Camille. But I know you're not calling me her name while you're fuckin' me ... or are you?"

"See, comments like that is the reason why you'll never be my main bitch."

"So who's your main? Is it Camille?"

"Shut the fuck up. You're throwing off my focus."

Tre Pound was staring down at his dark dick as he slid it back and forth along her light-skinned back, squishing her ass cheeks together to give his member comfort, trying to strengthen it. This was the first time he'd had trouble staying aroused while he fucked her. And he knew it was because he was comparing her to Camille.

Buttercup was light-skinned. Camille was too but a shade or two deeper into brown. Buttercup had large breasts and a perfectly rounded big ass; Camille had titties—perky half-handfuls that stayed firm when you squeezed them—but her booty was just as perfect as Buttercup's, just a smaller type of perfect.

Tre Pound couldn't focus.

"What are you doing?" Buttercup asked. "You need some help?"

"I'm good. Hold on."

But Buttercup turned around anyway. She placed her hands on his chest, guiding him onto his back. With a soft palm, she took ahold of his manhood and started stroking him. Jerking him. He started to harden up, and the veins that webbed through his shaft began to bulge.

"There we go," Buttercup said, smiling. "Almost where I need him."

Flipping her hair over her shoulder to one side, she dipped her head and sucked on the topmost skin of his dick—just the tip; though her bottom lip hung a smidge lower. Then she smacked her lips as she suddenly released him. She did this several times, teasingly. Suck*Smack*Release. Suck*Smack*Release. It felt incredible and weakening, vulgar and excessive. A thought entered Tre Pound's mind that he immediately regretted: *I wonder how Camille's lips would feel if she learned this. I could teach her.*

"We're making progress," Buttercup announced. "I think someone's about to cum."

She hummed that last part: *about to cuuuum.* Soothing hot breath came with it. It made Tre Pound shiver, and it seemed as though that was her intent.

"I'm sorry for stabbing you," she said, then deep-throated him while sucking her cheeks in. She pulled back and stopped at the tip. "Did you hear me?"

"Apology accepted," Tre Pound said with his eyes closed.

"Even though I think you deserved to get stabbed, I'm still sorry. I let my love for you get the best of me."

"It's okay, Camille."

Buttercup sighed, but she still kept pleasing him, talking in between every mouthful. "I need to stop worrying about ... who you're sleeping with and enjoy ... what I have now." Suck*Smack*Release. "Sitting in jail made me think ... about being happy for what I have and not being mad about what I don't."

She sat up so she could jack him off again. She started slow, evening out the clear film. Then she spit on it and evened that out too. Her hand was gliding now. She jerked faster, so fast her voice began to vibrate.

"They're gonna give me probation because you didn't show up for court. Thank you for not showing up, I knew you wouldn't. While I was in there, I kept asking myself: Why did I try to kill that man? Is it because I felt like you used me? Then I thought about it: I'm trying to use you for my own needs; you just won't let me use you how I wanna use you. I was mad because I was losing the battle of who's using who, when I should have been happy to have the freedom to choose whoever I want to be with."

"Stop pulling so hard," said Tre Pound.

Buttercup slowed down. Gentle strokes, tighter pressure. "When you showed up at my job with that brown-skinned little girl ... that's what it was. That's what set me off. I thought you were throwing her in my face.

Look who has your spot, Buttercup. Should've tried harder and this young ho wouldn't have bumped you to the side. That's what it felt like you were saying to me."

Lithely, Buttercup swung her leg over him and straddled him. She guided him inside her, then grabbed onto the headboard and grinded her pussy circularly. She bounced a couple times, but mostly just passionate circles. Tre Pound ran his hands up her stomach, across the grooves of her ribs and squeezed her sexy breasts.

"I love you," she said. "And I promise I won't try to kill you no more."

"I won't let you."

"And if I feel like I'm getting tired of waiting on you to make me number one, I won't get mad. I'll just leave, okay?"

"Whatever you wanna do, do that shit."

"But I have a feeling you're gonna realize how much I love you. You're gonna see those other bitches for who they are—bitches. I'm gonna be all you need, all you ever need, and I'm gonna give you solace when there's nowhere else to turn, give you shelter from all harm, and give you Buttercup Denise in her purest form."

"Give me that shit now."

Tre Pound loved Buttercup's soft skin but it wasn't enough. He couldn't cum. No matter how hard he tried, no matter how wet her pussy got or how close he was to climaxing, he couldn't quite *get there*. It was frustrating because he knew the reason why. He wanted her to be Camille. He wanted her breasts to not be so big, her body to slim down just a little bit more—almost boney, but enough pounds to still feel tender flesh when he gripped her hips. He wanted her to whisper in his ear what Camille said to him on the highway that day: *It's big. Hard. I knew you wanted me bad too.* He wanted Buttercup to hold his face with smaller hands and kiss him with more lust.

The sad thing was he wasn't even sure if that would work.

He needed the real thing.

Chapter 10

After straightening out his steering wheel, Tre Pound geared the Infiniti M into park. He looked at his dash, at all the technology crammed into the small control panel and thought about the craftsmen who put it all together. *They built this for me,* Tre Pound said to himself. *All these safety features surrounding me, protecting me. They built this for me.*

He pushed the audio button just to see the system elegantly power down.

Leaning forward, he looked up at Bernice's house. Up and to the right, he saw Camille's bedroom window. It was dark, curtains closed. She was probably sleep.

Good.

Tre Pound got out and went inside.

"Where you been at?" Bernice asked Tre Pound when he walked through the door. She said it spitefully, as if he were one of her sons. "It's 2 o'clock in the morning. Nobody comes in my house at this time of night but me."

"I was at a friend's house, auntie."

"You smell like pussy. If you're gonna be staying here, I won't allow you to be out all night fucking your little groupie girlfriends and then walk in here when you feel like it. At this house there are rules. You stayed here before when you was younger. You know the rules. Ain't shit changed."

"My bad, auntie."

Bernice leaned into Tre Pound quickly, and his first thought was she was about to hug him. Instead, she started patting him down. He stepped away from her, chuckling.

"What the hell?" Tre Pound said.

"Do you have a gun?" Bernice asked him.

"Yeah, I got a gun."

"You don't remember my rules?"

"Yeah, but I'm grown now, auntie. You know I got a crazy lifestyle. Last couple times I didn't have my heat on me, I almost got killed. A chick tried to set me up at her house not too long ago."

"If you think you need a gun in this house, then you don't need to be in this house."

"Cutthroat had guns in this house."

"Cutthroat was my man!" she said angrily. "Are you my man?! 'Cause if you are, there's bills that need to be paid and plumbing that needs to be fixed, shingles that need to be put on the roof."

"Nah, I'm not yo man, auntie."

"I didn't think so. Put that gun in yo car. Put it wherever you want to but not in here. You will obey me in this house."

Tre Pound turned and went back outside. He took his pistol out and looked at the chrome slide-action barrel as it twinkled under the moonlight. He couldn't will himself to sleep without it. It was too unsafe. Not just for him, but for everybody inside the house.

Someone called his name.

"Tre Pound."

He looked up. It was Camille, leaning out the window in a droopy tank top with a burnt orange sports bra underneath. Her hair was uncombed.

"Throw it up here," she said, then clapped her hands twice. "Throw it. I'll catch it."

It took him a second to realize she was talking about his gun. He shook his head no. "Nah, I'ma just ride out. I'm about to hit up a hotel."

"If you leave, I'm going with you. You're not leaving me here with that bitch Bernice."

Tre Pound thought about what would happen if he and Camille stayed in the same hotel room overnight. If she tried something, he wasn't sure if he'd be able to resist.

"You better not drop it," he said, standing under the window.

"I won't. Throw it."

Tre Pound gave it a toss. She caught it.

When he walked back in the house, he saw Bernice sitting at the dining room table smoking a cigarette, staring off into space. Her leg was shaking underneath the table nervously. Something was wrong.

Tre Pound didn't bother to ask her what. He went upstairs, where Camille was holding her bedroom door open. She waved him in quickly, like they were partners in some kind of break-in. Tre Pound shook his head. *Dramatic bighead girl,* he thought.

"She been acting like a bitch for the last three hours," Camille said, shutting him inside the room. "I tried to hide in here and she came banging on the door talking about I left the kitchen light on. I'm not sure if I did or not, but don't be blaming me bitch."

There was a pallet on the floor that consisted of a thin sheet, a twin-sized comforter and two pillows. Tre Pound wondered if she put it together that quick, from the time he threw her up the gun till he came upstairs. He sat down on it and unstrapped the Velcro on his Reeboks, slipping each shoe off.

"What got her upset?" he asked.

"Shelton called her."

"What he say?"

"I don't know exactly what was said because she didn't have it on speakerphone. I was listening in from the top of the stairs and she was talking to him in the kitchen. But I could tell it was about money. I think she was asking him for some cash and he told her ass no."

"That doesn't make sense. She knows Shelton needs all the money he can get."

"She's a greedy bitch that don't got no hustle. That's what my momma used to say about her. My momma didn't like her at all. She said Bernice got pregnant by my daddy because he had money. She ain't never had a real job. After Daddy got killed, she was living off his life insurance policy. I guess that ran out and Shelton's been taking care of her lately. I heard her tell him, 'I know you got some cash stashed somewhere.'"

"That's cold-blooded."

"I should've beat her ass for asking him that. And now that she's not being taken care of, she's taking it out on everybody else. She smacked Seneca for leaving his shoes in the front room. I wish she would put her hands on me."

Tre Pound rolled his socks off then pulled his T-shirt over his head. Bare-chested, he unbuckled his belt and tugged it off but kept his jeans on.

"You need some lotion?" Camille asked.

"Nah, I'm good."

"Yeah, you do," she joked.

He laid down on the pallet, pulling the comforter up to his abdomen so the gun tucked in his waist would be covered up in case Bernice walked in. *She got me hiding my damn gun,* he thought. *I forgot how evil she is.*

Tre Pound could recall when he was a kid, eight or nine years old, and he'd visit this house. All his life he never saw Bernice work. Never saw her earn her own income. Yet she had the ego and self-conceit of a breadwinner.

"Guess who called me today?" Camille said.

"Go to sleep."

"Krystal called me. From juvenile detention."

"She's still in there?"

"She sure is. I told her ass to run with me when we were in Shelton's house. Those people don't care who all they lock up when they're after somebody. And for somebody like Shelton, they'll throw everybody in jail just to nab him."

"They're gonna hold her till his trial is over, which could be a couple years."

"I told her that and she started crying. She was crying most of the conversation. She's not built for jail."

"Nobody is."

Camille fluffed her pillow and laid down close to the edge of the bed so she could look down at Tre Pound. "Moses called me again too."

"No bond?"

"Nope. He said he probably won't get one. He thinks he can maybe get them to come down to 10 years."

"He should take that if they offer it to him."

"I think so too. He got caught with a whole kilo of cocaine, didn't he?"

"That's what they say."

"He asked about you sending him some more money. I told him you might not be able to because Shelton got jammed up and we're all scrambling to get cash together."

"I'll still send him something."

"He was pissed when I told him where Krystal was. He thinks there's an informant somewhere close."

"I think so too."

Tre Pound lifted his shoulder in the motion of turning on his side, turning away from Camille. He was thinking about Moses, his last real homie left. Surely by now Moses had found out about the fallout between Tre Pound and Marlon. He had to know. News traveled faster in jail than it did on the streets.

For certain, fence-straddling wouldn't be allowed. Either you were with Tre Pound, or against him. Moses would have to choose sides when he got out.

"Krystal and Moses are gonna start sending their letters here," Camille shared. "Since Krystal is in juvenile, she can't receive letters from an inmate in an adult institution. That's their policy. So they're both gonna mail 'em here for me to re-mail 'em to them. I think that's a good idea, don't you? That's love. Love is strong stuff, ain't it? That's all they have right now. I can't wait for their letters to get here. I wanna read what they write to each other. Is that wrong?"

Tre Pound was silent.

"You still awake?" she asked.

He remained still, pretending. *Take yo ass to sleep,* he thought.

Chapter 11

Shelton had already started unbuttoning his orange jumper before the correctional officer told him to. He had a visit from his lawyer, Carlo Masaccio, and he wanted to get the strip search done as soon as possible so he could get his visit started. He was hoping for good news.

"You ain't gotta do that," the guard said.

Shelton stopped unbuttoning. "No squat and cough?"

"No, sir. I know who you are. You're Shelton King. I know you wouldn't try to sneak nothing in jail or out. Plus, I just come here for a paycheck. I try to see as less body parts as I have to, you know?"

Shelton nodded, then buttoned his jumper back up.

Since he'd been here at the Jackson County Detention Center, he was learning just how many people knew that he was Shelton King. Those who hadn't known who he was prior to his incarceration had found out from the constant media coverage. His case was high-profile, national news.

And he was getting mixed treatment from the staff here. Some correctional officers made him go through the whole rigmarole and beyond—stick your tongue out, lift your tongue up, lift it up more, lift your ball sack, squat, spread your cheeks, wider, I said wider Mr. King *wider*, cough, cough louder, now hurry up and get dressed. The C.O.'s either wanted to make their presence known to him in a good way, or a bad way.

Shelton shook his lawyer's hand and sat down across from him.

"Bad news," said Carlo Masaccio, straight to the point. "We have an informant."

Shelton didn't blink. "Who?"

"Maurice King."

"Gutta?!" Shelton shouted. "My fuckin' little brother?! Nah nah, I need proof, Carlo. Show me proof."

"You know I wouldn't show up without it, Mr. King."

As his lawyer unclipped his briefcase and got the paperwork ready, Shelton's fingers were tapping on the table anxiously. He started thinking backwards, first back to a few weeks ago, then further back through the past few months, then years. He couldn't find any memory of what he could have done wrong to Gutta to make him turn State against him. Still tapping, he waited for his lawyer to tell him it was a mistake.

But the paperwork Carlo laid out looked irrefutable.

"It seems that Maurice King signed on as a confidential informant four years ago," said Carlo, pointing to the date in the upper righthand corner of the affidavit.

The paperwork had an official Missouri seal on it, along with a mugshot of Gutta when he was more muscular. The photo had to have been taken in his strong-arm robbery days, around the time when he got engaged to Michelle, before Shelton started King Financial.

"It was part of a deal to get him out of a prison sentence," Carlo continued, "that stemmed from him assaulting a community activist. He chased the activist down with his vehicle and—"

"Pistol-whipped him," Shelton said, finishing his sentence. "He did it because the activist had announced where one of my dope houses was located, announced it on FM radio. I told Gutta not to touch him. And after it happened, I offered to pay Gutta's legal fees. He declined. I guess now we know why. He didn't want me to find out he turned State."

"Along with you, he cooperated against ..." Carlo started reading from the third paragraph, which was highlighted yellow. "... Tommy Nichols and Tony Nichols. Also he helped authorities catch Marlon Hayes and Moses Walker, as well as other known criminal operators from several different Kansas City neighborhoods, including 12th Street, 51st Street, 43rd Street, 27th Street and 72nd." He set the paper down. "Your brother made some big busts, but your arrest was his coup de grace. He's no longer obligated to participate in the C.I. program. He's been released."

Shelton was actually starting to feel better about the news. There were no gray areas. It was cut and dry. And Shelton knew exactly what options he had.

But Carlo Masaccio wasn't finished.

"There's more," Carlo said. He reached in his briefcase, bending back the interior leather slip pocket, and pulled out a mini cassette recorder. "On this tape is audio implicating you in the murder of Derrick 'Drought Man' Weber. At the end, there's a little more that you might find ... disturbing. This tape is a copy obtained from the FBI field office here in Kansas City."

Shelton tensed. "Play it," he said.

Carlo pressed the button. *Click.*

The tape crackled with static, but then six seconds in Tre Pound's voice came on. Shelton's heart immediately started beating faster. He expected to hear Gutta's voice. He leaned forward with his elbows on the table, listening closely.

" What the fuck was you thinkin'? You had everybody worried to death lookin' for you! You need yo ass beat or some boot camp ..."

Shelton recognized the voice a little late. It was Tre Pound on the recording. He was yelling at somebody

Then he heard a young girl speak. *" You probably wasn't worried about me. Yall just want me back in captivity. Yall don't love me.*

Shelton's spine went rigid. *That's Camille's voice,* he thought, alarmed. He bit his bottom lip and kept listening.

" You tryna tell me yo brother don't love you? Get the fuck outta here."

" He don't. He always workin' and ain't never got time for me. But he'll make time when he feels like bossing me around."

The two were arguing about who loved who in the family. Nonsense, Shelton thought. He looked at his lawyer quizzically. *How is this incriminating?*

"Here it comes," Carlo Masaccio said, reading his expression. "Just keep listening."

On the tape, Camille complained that her own mother didn't love her. Then, in a tone soused in empathy, Tre Pound revealed to her that her mother was dead. Camille started crying—it was a heartbroken sob that had Shelton feeling emotions he didn't want to feel right now, almost made him stop the tape. But then Camille blamed Tre Pound for her death, and that accusation led to the reason why this tape was so important.

" You can stop lying now. Trial's over. You won. But everybody know you did it. You can deny it all you want to.

Why did my momma have to die over some shit you did?"
" I didn't kill Drought Man!" Tre Pound's voice shouted.
" Oh yeah? Who did it then? If you didn't do it then you should know who did."
Then Camille's voice again: *" So who did it? Yeah, nobody but you. What's that look supposed to mean? I still know you did it."*
And then it fell out of Tre Pound's mouth: *" Shelton killed Drought Man."*
Shelton leaned back and let out the biggest sigh ever, as if he'd been holding his breath the whole time. Then he started biting his thumbnail nervously, as he started doing some thinking, strategizing, trying to figure out how the fuck he was going to fix this. He wasn't mad at Tre Pound, just disappointed. But Gutta ... that was a different story.
"Here comes the part that's unsettling," said Carlo Masaccio. "It shocked me, to say the least."
Shelton kept biting his nail, even tore a little bit of skin on the tip of his thumb. He let the tape play. And he got startled when he heard Camille scream:
" No! I need you!"
Then he heard shuffling sounds like they were wrestling. Then wet lip sounds—kissing? Did he hear a moan?
"What's happening?" Shelton asked.
Carlo Masaccio turned the volume up.
" I don't love you like this, Camille," Tre Pound was heard saying.
Next, Camille said, *" Yes, you do."*
" Get back in yo seat before we both do something' we both gon' regret."
" Make me. You can't, can you?"
" Camille, please ..."

" Put it in me. "

Shelton winced as he listened to them having sex. He was still staring at the tape a full minute after it stopped.

"Mr. King, your thumb is bleeding," said Carlo Masaccio.

It was like Shelton didn't even hear him. He kept biting his nail, nibbling harder. *Crunching.* He couldn't understand why his little sister and Tre Pound had fucked each other. This was the worst blow to the King family name.

Chapter 12

"Tre Pound, telephone. It's Shelton."

Pulling the covers from over his head, Tre Pound rubbed his eyes and saw Cash standing over him holding out a cell phone. He sat up, took the phone and yawned a big one before putting the phone up to his ear.

"Hello?"

"Good morning," Shelton said.

"Wussup, fam."

"I'm using Mr. Masaccio's cell phone so I can't talk long. Did you sleep good?"

Tre Pound looked down at the indent in his stomach, right beside his hairy navel. The hammer on his pistol had been poking him all night.

"I feel halfway rested," he said.

"Cash told me you slept on the floor in Camille's room. Why'd you sleep there? There was a bed in the room downstairs."

"You know Camille. She wants you to sleep where she wants you to sleep. She had a pallet set up as soon as I came upstairs."

Shelton paused. "Hmph." Then he said, "I found out who got me jammed up on this case."

"Who?" Tre Pound said quickly. He started putting on his socks. "You know I got you taken care of. Just give me a name."

"It was Gutta."

"Who? Which Gutta?"

"The Gutta that we both call family. My brother, yo cousin. He's been an informant for a long time now. But as of my arrest, he's been released from the C.I. program. I was his last bust. I know you're fucked up behind it, Tre Pound. I can hear it in your breathing. But he has to be treated like any other rat. He's not a King anymore. I don't care what his legal last name says. He's not a King. You hear me?"

Tre Pound was suddenly worried about all the shit he told Gutta over the years. All the shit about his homeboys, about the two murders Shelton committed, about the robberies he did himself. Everything Tre Pound and Gutta talked about in casual, private conversation was now compromised. Questions started running through Tre Pound's head a mile a minute: *Did Gutta turn in Marlon because I told him where he got his guns, did he get Moses caught because I told him where—and what time!—Moses was copping his first kilo, did Shelton get charged with Drought Man's murder because I told Gutta I didn't do it and that Shelton did?*

It was too much to be a coincidence.

And it was probably only a matter of time before charges got brought up on Tre Pound.

His heartbeat quickened. He looked up at Cash, who was waiting for his phone back. Cash looked upset, sort of sad. Shelton must have already told him what Gutta had done. He knew what Gutta's fate would be.

"Did you hear me?" Shelton asked.

"Yeah, I heard you," Tre Pound said, snapping back into the conversation. Guilt made him say, "I'll holla at Hoodey then. If you set it up, I'll meet up with him to get the money. As much as I hate to deal with that muthafucka, I'll get it done."

"No, I'm still having Gutta do it. He should be with Hoodey right now. I need you, Cash, and Seneca to meet up with Gutta and get the money from him. Then I need all of yall to have one big family talk."

In other words: *I need yall to kill the shit out of Gutta's ass.*

"We'll make it happen," Tre Pound said.

"I have faith that yall will. Cash and Seneca already know wussup. I'm not too sure if Seneca will take what's goin' down too well. Watch him. If you can, make him do the 'talking.' It'll toughen him up."

"A'ight."

Shelton said he had to go. Tre Pound hung up and gave Cash his cell phone back.

"Call Gutta and see where he's at," Tre Pound said to Cash. "See if he has the money yet. I gotta get dressed."

"Okay," Cash said, and he started walking out of the room.

"Cash."

"Yeah?"

"You a'ight?"

Tre Pound could only imagine what was going through Cash's 17-year-old mind. He had a serious responsibility weighing on his shoulders. He had to participate in his big brother's murder.

"I'm good," Cash said, then he left the room.

Tre Pound pulled out his gun and looked at it, his thumb rubbing gingerly over the black checkered grip. This was what he would use to kill Gutta if Seneca couldn't pull the trigger. Tre Pound checked the clip, popped it back in and cocked the hammer back.

The sound made Camille stir in her sleep. Tre Pound got up and pulled on his shirt, trying to hurry up and leave before she woke up.

He wasn't fast enough.

"Where are you going?" Camille asked, sitting up in her bed.

"Handle some business."

"You going to see a girl?"

Tre Pound put his Reeboks on and laced them up tight. Then he looked over at Camille. Her eyes were still low—almost closed—and red from sleep. He wondered why her first waking thought was a jab about him seeing a girl. Looking closely, he saw that she had slobber dried up in the corners of her mouth. Wild strands of hair had fountained over her forehead in accidental bangs.

She looked homely.

But she was still beautiful.

"Wash yo face first before you get in my business," Tre Pound said on his way out the door. "Tre block."

Chapter 13

Tre Pound looked in his rearview mirror at his upraised trunk. Gutta had just walked to the back to throw the duffel bag of money inside. Cash and Seneca were sitting in the back seat.

"Are yall ready?" Tre Pound asked the two boys in a low, stern voice. "This has to be done. Shelton said so. It's the only way Shelton will even have the possibility of getting his freedom back or getting a good deal in court."

"I'm ready," said Cash.

Seneca was still staring out the back passenger window. His cheeks were so chubby that Tre Pound couldn't tell if he was pouting or not.

"Seneca, are you ready?" Tre Pound asked him directly.

Seneca turned slowly. He blinked twice at Tre Pound, lost for a second, then turned back and started staring out the window again. "I guess I'm ready," he shrugged.

The trunk slammed closed, as Gutta was on his way back inside the car.

"You better start looking ready then," Tre Pound hissed at him. "Straighten yo face, lil cuzz. We don't want him to think something' is up."

"How am I supposed to look? You want me to smile?"

"Stop looking out the fuckin' window like you lost a puppy!" Tre Pound flared. "If he gets any idea of what's about to happen, he knows how to—"

Tre Pound stopped abruptly when Gutta opened the passenger door. He got in quickly and strapped on his seatbelt.

"So we're going to drop this money off to Mr. Carlo Masaccio?" Gutta asked Tre Pound. "You know where to meet him?"

"Yeah," Tre Pound said, pulling off.

A couple minutes into the drive, Gutta turned and looked in the back seat.

"What yall so quiet for?" he asked his little brothers, smiling. "This is a joyous occasion! Our bro is coming home!"

Tre Pound looked in the rearview to see what response the teens gave. Cash's lips curled up into a halfway believable smile. Seneca didn't even attempt. *After this is over,* Tre Pound thought, *I'ma smack that little nigga in his mouth.*

"You was right, Tre Pound," Gutta said. "The best thing I could've done was call the police about those bodies in my house. They're calling it like it was: self-defense."

"When it's cut and dry like that, they don't have a choice."

"You know back in the day, I would've dumped those bodies deep off in Swope Park. They wouldn't have found them niggas till next Spring."

"Yeah, that was the old Gutta."

Gutta laughed. "I'm still the same Gutta. I feel new and improved. Better than ever."

Tre Pound sensed a lot of excitement coming from Gutta. He was enthused, talkative, jittery. Those were the same signs Tre Pound had seen in people recently released from prison. In Gutta's case, he had been recently released from his informant status. He was amped up.

Soon, though, he would get cooled down.

Tre Pound drove around the back of a modest shopping center on Linwood that was still up and running, except for the two vacant spaces on the end. Tre Pound parked behind the last space, next to stairs that led up to a back door with rusted out hinges. The door was open. Seneca and Cash said they'd jimmied the lock this morning before Tre Pound even woke up. Shelton had them do it.

Shelton is teaching them to kill just like he taught me, Tre Pound thought.

"When did Carlo move to this office?" Gutta asked, skeptical.

"He hasn't moved in yet," Tre Pound told him. "It's still being renovated. He wanted us to meet him here so he could let in the drywall guys. Hopefully he's here."

Tre Pound got out the car, they all did, Seneca stepping out and shutting his door last. Tre Pound eyed him slyly. *Pull it together, Seneca.*

Cash must have picked up on Tre Pound's irritation. He tried to help out. "Seneca, get the money out the trunk," Cash snapped at him.

"What's wrong with him?" Gutta asked.

"He didn't want to get up this early," Cash answered.

Good lie, Tre Pound thought.

Gutta was the first one up the steps. He trotted up, full of energy. The rest of them fell in behind him, followed him inside.

"It looks like the remodelers got a long way to go," Gutta noticed.

One of the walls had one huge hole in it the size of a

massive 1500 gallon fish tank, and maybe one used to be here. There was another wall that was missing completely. Only the wood frame was in place, with insulation pressed between each board. Up on the ceiling was a brown circular stain. From a roof leak.

Click-clack.

Gutta turned around quickly.

Tre Pound was pointing his pistol at him.

"What the fuck is going on?" Gutta said.

Tre Pound kept his gun trained on him, but nodded at Seneca. "Go ahead, Seneca."

Seneca pulled his .380 from his waist and pointed it at Gutta, who took a step back and raised his hands in apology. There was fear in Gutta's eyes. But he also had a heartsick look that said he knew why guns had been pulled on him.

"Shelton ordered this, didn't he?" Gutta said sadly.

"Pull the trigger!" Cash shouted.

Seneca was aiming at Gutta one-handed. He kept clenching his jaws, working himself up. A tear slid down his cheek.

"He's not a King anymore," Tre Pound said to Seneca. "You're killing a rat who snitched on Shelton."

"I'm sorry," Gutta said, near tears himself. "They made me do it."

"They can't make you do shit!" Tre Pound shouted. "Can't nobody make a King do shit! You turned your back on yo family. For that, you gotta die. Ain't no more love, nigga."

"I never told on you, though, Tre Pound. Never. I helped them get a lot of people but not you. They couldn't make me do that and believe me they tried. I love you, nigga. I love all of yall."

"You used me, didn't you? All the shit we used to stay up and talk about. All the street shit I told you! Nigga, you used me!"

"I did what the fuck I had to do!" Gutta shouted back, a sudden change of attitude. He was angry. "You think I wanted to be an informant? You think I liked doing that shit? I did what I had to do. And now I gotta live with that shit for the rest of my—"

Bang!

Seneca shot him in the chest and he fell back hard on the unfinished flooring. Gutta cried out, tried to grab a board near him to either help himself back up or sling it at them. He never got a chance. Tre Pound walked up on his fallen body and shot him between the eyes.

Gutta was dead.

Tre Pound looked over at Seneca. "If you can get up close on your man after you shoot him, do it. Always try and guarantee your kill."

Seneca was just staring at Gutta's corpse. The blood underneath him was dark and oily. It was growing, the red streams snaking toward the walls. Tre Pound stepped back so the blood wouldn't bump his foot, then he walked over to Seneca and put his hand on his shoulder.

"Wipe those tears," Tre Pound said.

Seneca did, swiping each eye with his palm.

"Why are you shedding tears for a snitch?"

"I'm not," Seneca said, sniffling.

"Well, why are you crying?"

"Because it's not over."

"What's not ov—?"

Click-clack.

Cash had cocked his pistol and aimed it at the back of Tre Pound's head.

"Get his gun," Cash said to Seneca.

It was pretty clear what was happening. Tre Pound knew how Shelton's mind worked. Shelton told Cash and Seneca to kill Gutta *and* Tre Pound. Tre Pound had an idea why, but he wanted to know for sure.

"He told yall about what I said to Gutta about Drought Man?" Tre Pound asked, as Seneca took his gun from him. "He told yall to kill me for that?"

"He didn't say nothing about you talking' to Gutta," Cash said. "He's disappointed about what you said to Camille. About what you did to her. About what you did to our little sister!"

Said to Camille? Tre Pound thought, puzzled. *Did to her? What are they talking about? I know Camille didn't tell them what happened on the side of the highway ...*

"Shelton must have gotten some misinformation. I didn't say or do shit to Camille. Yall know that."

"Shelton told us what happened. You told her he killed Drought Man. You told her everything in the car on the side of the highway."

Fuck! Tre Pound cursed himself silently. *How did Shelton find out?* If Shelton knew about that, then he had to know about—

"You fucked her too," Cash said angrily. "That's the part I didn't even understand. If you wouldn't have done that, Shelton would have let you live. *I* would have let you live!"

"If you think I fucked Camille, you gotta be crazy," said Tre Pound. He wanted to turn around and face Cash but he knew he wouldn't let him. *When you have the advantage, keep the advantage,* Cutthroat always said. And Tre Pound had instilled that in Cash and Seneca long ago.

"It was on tape!" Cash shouted from behind him. "You were recorded on audio by the FBI. They're using the tape against Shelton."

Damn. Why did I fuck Camille? Stupid, Tre Pound. Fucking stupid!

There was nothing he could do now but deny it.

"That's the silliest shit I ever heard. I would never fuck Camille," Tre Pound lied. "C'mon now, yall know that shit. Like I said, this is misinformation. Cash, stop playing around. Put that gun down. Seneca, give me my gun back."

Seneca actually started to hand it back. Until Cash snatched it from him.

"What the hell are you doing?!" Cash barked at Seneca.

"He said he didn't do it," Seneca replied in a pitiful tone.

"Shelton told us he would try to lie. But they got the shit on tape, Seneca. He's a creep and a snake. Even Marlon told us that."

Tre Pound squeezed his eyes shut, trying to erase all the stupid shit he'd done over the past few years. And fucking Camille was the biggest of them all.

"Now stand back here and shoot this nigga in the back of his head like Shelton told you to. You don't wanna disobey Shelton, do you?" Cash stepped away and Seneca took his place.

Tre Pound really-really wanted his gun back.

Click-clack.

The sound made Tre Pound flinch.

Seneca raised the gun to the back of his head.

"Do it!" Cash said.

"Seneca, realize what you're doing," Tre Pound warned him. "Remember who's always believed in you?

Me, that's who. Not Shelton, not Gutta, not Cash, but *me*."

"Tell him to shut the fuck up, Seneca."

"The person who is telling me to shut the fuck up is the same person who's been leaving you at home lately. I'm always there for you. Always have been."

"If you don't do it, I'ma do it. And then I'ma tell Shelton."

Tre Pound chuckled. "You hear that, Seneca. He's gonna tell Shelton. He's gonna tell on you."

Seneca placed the muzzle on the back of Tre Pound's neck.

"Shelton's not the real head of the King family," Tre Pound said. "I am. I've been keeping our name relevant, not Shelton. Yall need to be obeying me. Seneca, put that gun down. *Now.*"

"He fuckin' raped Camille," Cash said. *"He raped yo sister, Seneca."*

Tre Pound said, "What do you think yo brothers are gonna do to you when they find out what you did to Camille? Huh, Seneca? They're gonna smoke you too. You might be next on the kill list after me."

Out of the corner of his eye, Tre Pound could see Cash staring at Seneca. Cash must have seen something suspicious in Seneca's expression.

"What the fuck is he talking' about?" Cash asked. "Seneca, did you do something' to Camille?"

"Tell him what happened," Tre Pound said. "But he probably already knows."

"Fuck what he's talking' about," Cash said angrily. "Seneca, did you fuck Camille too?!"

Suddenly, Seneca turned the gun on Cash. Instinctively, Cash started to lift his weapon but Seneca pulled the trigger.

Bang!

The bullet's impact pushed Cash backwards. *Bang! Bang! Bang!* Three more shots before he fell to the ground. Seneca then walked up on his brother's body and shot him between the eyes.

"That's exactly how it's done," Tre Pound said, draping his arm over Seneca's shoulder. They stared at the body together. "If you wouldn't have did him, he would've did you."

Seneca started shaking. He was crying, trying to hold it in. The tears rolled down his big cheeks. Tre Pound took his arm off his shoulder and went and had a seat on a re-sealed five-gallon bucket of paint.

He lit up a cigarette and watched his little cousin Seneca cry, as he thought about how close he came to being murdered. In a way, Tre Pound was proud of his cousins—both Seneca and Cash—for having the discipline to follow through with a plan that Shelton laid out. They were able to toss aside feelings and history and memories and focus on what needed to be done. Tre Pound wasn't sure if he would have been ready to kill a family member at their age.

Tapping his ashes on the floor, he took another long drag. He blew the stream out with his lips puckered, trying to form smoke O's. His nerves were starting to calm down.

"We'll clean their bodies up in a minute," Tre Pound said. "Just let me finish this cigarette."

Chapter 14

Early afternoon, Camille was still sitting on her bed in the clothes she slept in—loose tank top over her sports bra and small gym shorts. She didn't want to leave her room since all the guys were gone and she was here by herself with Bernice. She was glad when her friend Krystal called her.

"Have you heard any good news yet?" Camille asked.

"They haven't told me when they're gonna let me go." Krystal said it worriedly, as if she was convinced she might not ever get released. "I can't do this anymore, Camille. I can't. These girls in here are evil!"

"Hang in there, Krystal. They can't hold you past Shelton's trial. You know that. Just don't give them any information on Shelton."

"I don't know anything!"

"I know you don't. But they'll try to get you to make up shit. You better not do that. Because them threatening you won't be as bad as what Shelton and Tre Pound will do to you, and I can't save you from them. Just hang tight."

"Camille, this is illegal. It has to be. I didn't do anything! I tried to explain it to the caseworker and she's acting like she can't do nothing. They're holding me hostage."

Camille felt bad for her. She honestly thought she would end up in jail before Krystal. Krystal was the good girl out of all of them, the one that tried to keep everybody else out of trouble. Krystal was a people pleaser. And those were the worst qualities to have in there.

"You gotta toughen up," Camille said. "Whining about it won't get you outta there. I told yo ass to keep running with me when we was at my brother's. Now look what happened."

Krystal took a deep breath. "Did you get me and Moses' letters yet?"

"Not yet, no."

The phone clicked. Camille told Krystal to hold on for a sec so she could click over, thinking it was Tre Pound, *hoping* it was Tre Pound. Instead, when she clicked over she got a voice-automated system, the I'm-in-jail voice-automated system. She sprang up off her bed, not wanting it to be Tre Pound anymore.

She listened for a name.

"... call from ... Moses Walker."

Camille accepted the call. "Hey, Moses!"

"Wussup, sweet thang," Moses said.

Camille smiled. She liked Moses' voice. He was always in a good mood, no matter what was going on. Maybe he could rub some of it off on Krystal.

"I got your girlfriend on the other line. You want me to merge the call?"

"Hell yeah."

Camille connected them.

"Hello?" Moses said.

"Hello?" Krystal said excitedly. "Moses?!"

"Yeah, it's me. Man, it's good hearing your voice. I miss you."

"I miss you too baby!"

"Hang in there, you hear me? Don't let that place keep you down."

"I'm trying to, Moses. But it's hard. These people here are crazy. I don't think I'll be able to make it as long as you."

"If I can make it, you can make it. In the letter I wrote you, I tried to give you some tips on how to survive in there. Camille, did you get our letters yet, mine or Krystal's?"

"Not yet."

"Well, Krystal, when you get my letter, study it. Okay?"

"Okay," Krystal said.

"I love you."

"I love you too, Moses."

Camille was amazed at their love for each other. Their love was so strong, it was holding up from miles apart, through barbed wire fences and brick walls. Camille wanted that type of love one day.

"Camille!" Bernice shouted from downstairs.

I hate when she calls my name, Camille thought.

Sighing, Camille put the phone in her neck and yelled, "What?!"

"Get yo ass down here and find out what!"

You ain't my momma. Don't talk to me like that, ho.

Camille put the phone back up to her ear and started to tell Camille and Krystal to hold on but they were so engrossed in lovey-dovey conversation that they probably wouldn't notice she was gone. She put the phone down on her bed and stormed out her room.

Standing in the foyer, Bernice was waiting with her arms crossed. There was something tucked underneath one arm, looked like two envelopes. Then she held them up, flapping them back and forth. "You got mail coming here?" she asked accusingly.

"Yes, I do." Camille tried to grab them but Bernice pulled back.

"Did you ask me could you have mail coming here?"

"I didn't know I had to ask."

"When you have mail coming from prison you do. Who the fuck are these people?" Bernice read the return addresses. "Krystal Hamilton. Moses Walker. I don't want random criminals knowing where the hell I live."

"They're my friends. They're writing here because the jails they're in won't let them write each other."

"I don't give a shit! I'm putting these letters back in the mail, return to sender."

"No, you can't do that!"

"Watch me."

"Don't take it out on me because you're a broke-ass bitch that can't pay her own bills!" Camille snapped. "I heard you begging my brother for money so wipe that dumb look off yo face. Getting mad at me won't solve yo problems. Go get you a fuckin' job and earn—"

SMACK!

Bernice had backhanded her. "Don't you ever talk to an adult like that ever again in yo life!"

Camille was holding the side of her face. It stung. Then before she knew it, she smacked Bernice back.

***

Tre Pound waited until they got to Bernice's, until they were outside the car and the car doors were shut before he said what he wanted to say to Seneca. He pinched the arm of Seneca's shirt, pulling him close to the garage door.

"I couldn't say what I wanted to say to you on the ride over because my car is probably tapped. But all the tears and sorrow and all that other soft shit has got to stop. Gutta ain't coming back, Cash ain't coming back. So wipe them tears and I don't wanna see another one come down yo face. Man up, lil' nigga."

Seneca wiped his face with the bottom of his T-shirt.

"If yo momma ask where Cash is, tell her that him and Gutta went to take the money to Shelton's lawyer. That's all we know. Let people speculate after that, let 'em think they got robbed for the money. As far as me and you, we went to a female's house. A chick named Buttercup. She'll be our alibi if I tell her to."

"I got it," Seneca said.

"And don't ever talk about what happened today to nobody."

"I know, Tre Pound." Seneca wiped his face again. "Do I look okay?"

Tre Pound smiled. "You look like a gangsta. Here, take this." He pulled off his platinum chain with the crown pendant, and Seneca bowed his head gratefully as Tre Pound placed it around his neck. "It's yours. You earned that muthafucka."

Seneca hadn't looked up yet. He had his chin to his chest, staring down at the diamonds and angling the pendant to see them flicker but got nothing because they were standing in the shade. Still, he was awestruck. This was his Olympic medal. He looked up at Tre Pound, finally. "How long do I get to wear it?"

"Forever. It's yours, nigga. You're no longer my little cousin. We're brothers. You're little Tre Pound."

"I'm Tre Pound?"

"Yeah, if you wanna be."

"I do."

Tre Pound put his arm around Seneca and walked him in the house. He was telling him how proud he was and how everyone wasn't built for murder, when they stumbled upon the fight. Camille was on top of Bernice, punching her in the face in the living room. Bernice tried to cover up but she wasn't doing so good. Camille was nailing her—lazily though, as if she'd been sitting on Bernice for a while and her arms were tired.

Tre Pound pulled her off and she didn't resist.

"I want that bitch out of my house!" Bernice screamed, as Seneca helped her to her feet by her underarms. She couldn't get her footing. Seneca was having trouble holding her. "I want her out! Get her out!"

"I didn't wanna be here in the first place!" Camille yelled. "I bet you won't ever put yo hands on me again! I know that much!" She turned and stormed upstairs to pack her stuff.

Tre Pound followed her; he was on her tail fast. "What the fuck happened?"

"She got mad because I had Krystal and Moses' letters sent here." Camille swung her suitcase on her bed. "Then that bitch grew some balls and smacked me."

"She smacked you?"

"I told you she been gettin' beside herself since Shelton cut her funds. She's lucky I didn't fuckin' kill her. Why did yall leave me here with her?"

"So where are you going?"

"I don't know. Anywhere but here." She was stuffing clothes inside the suitcase, cramming them in, pushing down with both hands, flattening. She flopped the lid closed and barely got it zipped.

Tre Pound knew she was waiting on him to tell her he'd take her somewhere. She was stuffing grocery bags with clothes now, mumbling something about catching the bus out of town when Tre Pound knew damn well—and *she* knew damn well—that she'd never catch the bus on her own.

Tre Pound grabbed one of her bags, the least heaviest.

"We'll go to a hotel," he said.

Chapter 15

Tre Pound paid for a hotel room at Days Inn, located in south Kansas City on the east side of Blue Ridge Boulevard. Camille stuck her hand out when the clerk offered the key card. She wanted to be the one to find the room first.

She slid the card in the slot, pushed it open and went in, and Tre Pound was still coming down the outside tier with the duffel bag strap on his shoulder. *She's too fucking excited,* he thought.

When he got to the room, she was already sitting on one of the beds Indian-style, her fists balled in her lap. She smiled. "What took you so long?"

He went to the bathroom, stood on the toilet lid and removed a ceiling tile. He put the duffel bag in, scooted the tile back, had to tap it with the bottom of his fist so it would fall in place.

"Are you bonding Shelton out in the morning?" she asked when he laid down on the opposite bed.

Not a question he wanted to answer right now. He was hoping he and Seneca cleaned the vacant space good enough. There probably was still blood on the ground, but there was a chance it would get dusted over and overlooked in the remodeling. The bodies, as they decayed, would get found eventually. Just let some time go by and the smells of the dead would thicken, begin to stifle the air within. By that time, though, forensics would be harder to pull. He was sure he did good on the clean-up, though. No prints, no nothing.

He was pretty sure. Sort of sure. But with every murder there was always doubt.

"What's wrong?" Camille asked him.

He turned his head toward her. "We're not bonding Shelton out in the morning."

Her mouth dropped. "Why not?" She swung her legs off the bed, sitting closer to him but still on her side. "Yall didn't get the money?"

"We got it. It's in the duffel bag I just put in the bathroom."

"What's the problem then? They better let my brother out of that goddamn jail before I go down there and break him out."

Tre Pound turned his head again, staring back at the ceiling. "Shelton just tried to kill me."

"What?!"

"I'm not repeating myself."

"How did he try to kill you? That doesn't make sense. He's in jail. When did he try? Recently?"

"Today."

Tre Pound told her how Shelton's plot unfolded, not in the right order but starting with the part that was most important to him—Seneca pointing the gun at him. He spoke musingly, as if he was still absorbed in the moment, then thinking more about his new feelings for Shelton than getting the details of the events out. It was frustrating Camille. She had to scream questions at him to get the whole story.

She scooted over to his bed, so close that his shirt was stuck under her bottom. "Gutta is the snitch, okay I understand that. But why did he try to kill *you*?"

"Shelton heard the tape."

"What tape, Tre Pound?" She grabbed his chin, tried to force him to look at her. He smacked her hand away and glared at her—*don't ever touch my face again*—and then stared back at the ceiling. "Talk to me, Tre Pound. What tape?"

"The tape that got recorded by the FBI," he began. "The tape of us fucking on the side of the highway."

She gasped. That was it, though. A gasp. It reminded Tre Pound that he and she were in different positions. His life was in danger because Shelton had connections, but Camille was just ... Camille was okay. She was the little sister, the victim, the just-as-guilty girl whose part in all this would get overlooked because she was only 15 years old. She could gasp or act as shocked as she wanted, say anything she wanted to, *Oh no oh my God this is bad I can't believe this,* but it would just be concern and not real fear.

"Oh my God," she whispered.

Tre Pound snapped. "Why the fuck are you sitting so close to me?!"

"Sorry. I didn't know that was a rule." The springs creaked when she rose. "Does your new Infiniti M have a recording device in it too?"

"I don't know."

"I'm not getting back in that car. Fuck that shit."

Tre Pound thought about telling her his role in providing Gutta street-related information over the years. Technically, Tre Pound had dry snitched—he'd inadvertently cooperated with the law. It wasn't the same

104

as what Gutta had done, but it was an act you could get killed for. Shelton was justified all the way.

But if he told her, it would just be to hear her say that it wasn't his fault.

He couldn't tell her. Right now she had to feel halfway responsible for Shelton plotting to take his life. She jumpstarted the sex on the side of the highway, and if you added in the fact that his arm had been in a sling at the time, then it could be argued that he was defenseless when she forced herself on him.

Tre Pound's phone went off. He was still lost in thought until Camille told him it was ringing. He answered it.

"Hello?"

"You're on TV!"

Tre Pound jackknifed to a sitting position when he heard Seneca's excited statement. "What channel?" Tre Pound asked urgently.

"All of 'em!"

Grabbing the remote, Tre Pound clicked on the TV and found a news station. Weatherman in a suit and tie was pointing to a cold front moving north of Kansas City into St. Joseph, Missouri. Camille asked what was going on as he changed to another channel. He just barely missed his mugshot flash in the corner of the screen. Camille uttered an "Oh my God." He turned the volume up.

"I hope they catch that guy asap," said the blonde reporter. She was wearing pearls, and her eyes fell on her co-worker for assistance. "Right, Parks? We can't have that guy running around our streets."

"He's not an official suspect," said Parks, the anchorman. "Just a person of interest. The officers were killed at his residence after a report of a break-in so we can't really say if this guy is the guy. Our cops just need to talk to him." The screen went to a contact bulletin, but Parks' words could still be heard in a more formal voice: "If you have any information on Mr. Levour King's whereabouts, please contact—"

Tre Pound shut the TV off.

"That's bullshit!" Camille said. "You weren't even there! Marlon killed them, right?"

Tre Pound thanked Seneca for the heads-up and told him he'd talk to him later. He tried to hang up, but Seneca had a question.

"Where'd you and Camille go?" he asked.

"To a hotel. I'll talk to you later, Seneca."

"Tre Pound," Seneca corrected him. "You said I was Tre Pound now."

"Yeah, whatever. Later." Tre Pound hung up.

Camille was on her feet, pacing the room, complaining about how the news always tried to ruin somebody's image before they got the facts straight. "If you're just a person of interest," she said, "why'd they have to put your mugshot up there? Huh? Answer me that." Tre Pound had a different view, though. This was a good thing for him. Being a funk artist, this would put a little fear in the hearts of his enemies. Tre Pound the Cop Killer. Or Tre Pound the Double-Murder Cop Killer. As far as the courts and the judicial process, they would *never* find him guilty. He made the call to the police to the report the break-in from his own phone, which cell towers could corroborate if need be. If they charged him, it would be another murder case beat. Especially with Carlo Masaccio on his defense team again.

The only issue would be turning himself in as soon as possible. His uncle Cutthroat was killed by the police. Tre

Pound didn't want to get caught in the street and killed by a rogue cop.

He laid down on the bed and got comfortable with two pillows.

"Why are you smiling?" Camille asked.

"Because I know how the judicial system works."

"You don't think this is a big deal?"

"It is. But once I get Carlo on top of it, it won't be. And I got a million dollars in the bathroom for lawyer and investigator fees. This case won't do nothing but boost my popularity."

"You're not gonna use the money to get Shelton out?"

"You want him to kill me?"

"No." Camille laid down too. She grabbed two pillows just like him and faced him. "When are you gonna turn yourself in?"

"I don't know yet."

"You're not gonna give Hoodey his money back?"

"No siree Bob. If he wants his money back, he's gon' have to take it from me. And he ain't dumb enough to try that."

"I don't think you should be making any more enemies. Do you?"

"What's one more enemy? I don't give a fuck."

Camille put her hand on her stomach, watching her own thumb make circles against her shirt. "Tre Pound, I'm ..." She paused, so did her thumb. She eyed him. "If you had a son, do you think he would be safe with all the enemies you got?"

"Shut up and go to sleep," he said, rolling over so his back was to her.

He closed his eyes, thinking about Seneca's call. It was a quick scare. Good thing the news didn't pop up with his picture in connection to the murder of Gutta and Cash. For that, he'd probably have to really go on the run.

"I'm sorry," Camille said.

Tre Pound didn't want to hear it but asked anyway. "For what?"

"For trying to run away to Texas with Lil' Pat. For it leading up to what we did on the side of the highway. For loving you in a way that's not normal."

"You should be sorry," he said.

Chapter 16

Something was wrong. In the mirror, Tre Pound stared at the reflection of himself—handsome, of course—wearing a white button-up tucked into brown dress pants. And a tie. A red one. The strange thing was: He didn't know why he was dressed this way.

"You're crispy though, nigga," he said to his image. "You look good dressed up. You look better than Shelton."

He took the tie off and untucked his shirt.

Heading downstairs, he noticed he was still wearing wing-tipped dress shoes and decided to leave them on. The smell of breakfast wafted into him pleasantly as he hit the hallway, almost to the kitchen. He knew what was cooking—fried eggs, Italian sausage, toast (wheat toast, he hoped), bacon, and cinnamon oatmeal. He just didn't know *who* was cooking.

Then he saw her at the stove.

"Hey, Tre Pound, good morning," Camille said over her shoulder, then went back to stirring the pot of oatmeal as she poured milk into it, sparingly, tiny milliliter splats at a time. She was wearing an apron, but where it was tied around the back of her there was panties. An apron and panties. Her naked female back muscles curved down into those pretty blue, spicy low-rise panties. Her hair was pulled up into a breezy knot.

"What's goin' on?" Tre Pound asked suspiciously.

She put the milk down and turned, her blue underwear twisting as she put her hand on her hip. Her pose gave her butt more shape. "I'm cooking breakfast," she said as if he asked a stupid question. "Sit down. It's almost ready."

Unsure, Tre Pound slowly sat down at the kitchen table. He watched her cook, until movement to the right of him caught his eye.

A toddler crawled into the kitchen. A brown-skinned baby boy in a Winnie the Pooh diaper. There was a pot of honey on his butt, and the diaper *swish-swished* as he crawled under the table, paying Tre Pound no mind. Tre Pound leaned over to see where the kid was going. He passed through the legs of the chair, closing in on Camille's feet.

Whose baby are you? Tre Pound thought. He started to ask Camille but suddenly didn't want to know the answer.

"Get your son," Camille said, "and put him in his high chair for me, please?"

He stood up fast and took a step back from the table. His heartbeat was going crazy.

Camille turned again, one eyebrow raised curiously. "You okay?"

"Whose son is that?" Tre Pound asked, pointed down at the baby that was trying to pull himself up Camille's legs.

"Yours."

"No it's not!"

"Whose is it then?"

"You tell me. I just know it ain't mine."

Camille bent down, picked the baby up and plopped him on her hip. The bib of her apron hid her nipples, just barely. With a stretching neck, she gave the baby boy a big, sloppy moist kiss on its cheek. "He looks just like you." She started toward Tre Pound, to let him hold the baby, but when he put his hand out in a come-no-further gesture she stopped. And frowned. "Tre ..." she said admonishingly, as if he had insulted their child. "Tre .. hold your son. Take him."

"Don't bring that baby close to me," he warned. "What's goin' on, Camille? Whose house is this? Whose baby is that? What the fuck is goin' on?"

The baby started crying. Loud, then louder. Tre Pound backed away until he couldn't any more, until the cabinetry behind him stopped him. Camille bounced the baby on her hip and it quieted down.

She sighed, then explained. "This is our house. The good ol' federal government gave it to us as part of the witness protection program. You testified against Shelton, remember? This is your son," she said, bouncing the baby once. "Did you forget we had sex on the side of the highway? Jesus, Tre Pound. I know you have regrets—I do too—but don't deny your child. He has nothing to do with this."

Tre Pound watched in bewilderment as Camille put the child in his high chair and buckled him in. While adjusting the strap's loop-through for waist tightening, she spoke again.

"I'm not gonna get mad," she said, not looking at him, fumbling with the straps. "This isn't the first time you've denied him. Hopefully by the time you get home from work, you'll want to be daddy again. You better be. For your own sake. I'm not gonna get mad right now. I can't promise later. So go to your appointment before you're late, Tre Pound."

Appointment?

He looked down at his shirt and dress pants and the semi-gloss leather of his shoes. Then he looked at his watch, an Audemars Piquet timepiece he stole from a man he murdered. The diamonds said it was 8 o'clock in the morning. He was running late—how late, late to where, he didn't know; he just knew his heart suddenly thumped with anticipation. He was supposed to be somewhere.

Without knowing why, he raced toward the front door and almost lost his balance—damn slippery wing-tips against hardwood—on his way out the kitchen. He gained speed on the carpet in the hallway.

"Have a great day, honey!" Camille called out.

He burst out the front of the house, ran to the driveway, yanked open the driver's door of a Honda Civic and didn't ask why it was a Honda Civic but knowing it was his he got in and started it up and reversed out into the street, geared into drive and throttled it. He put on his seatbelt for no other reason than to stop the chiming.

He called Carlo Masaccio.

"How are you, Mr. Levour King?"

"Fuck you!" Tre Pound flared. "You set me up."

"How?"

"You got me in the witness protection program. Why the fuck am I in this shit?"

"You signed up for it."

"Bullshit."

"Look in your glove compartment."

Tre Pound glanced at it curiously, a couple times, before finally leaning over and dropping the door. He snatched the contract out and tried to read and drive at the same time. He saw his name, "I, Levour King, hereby" in his own signature. There was more below: *All crimes initiated against third parties have been dissolved in exchange for testimony in the aforementioned trial,* United States of America vs Shelton King ... *for personally appearing before Judge Lyons and providing evidences and facts which contributed to conviction, Levour King has been granted residency in the Witness Security Program (WITSEC) for a duration dependent on threat of life but not to exceed 40 years.*

Tre Pound threw the document out the window and the highway wind snatched it.

"I just unsigned it," Tre Pound said into the phone.

"It doesn't work like that," Carlo Masaccio told him. "You have to finish your tenure. Look at it this way: it beats going to prison, right? I told you I would keep you out of prison."

"Nah, this doesn't beat prison. This ain't my life. I don't want it. I'm not an everyday suit and tie muthafucka. Tell them I wanna retract my statement. Tell them I lied on Shelton."

"As your lawyer, I have to do what's in your best interest. And what I feel is in your best interest isn't leaving the program."

"I'm already gone."

Tre Pound hung up and kept driving, until the highway sign he was looking for appeared—35th Street Exit Only. A moment later he was turning onto Agnes. His home. He clicked his seat belt off and frowned at what he saw in the yard.

A For Sale sign.

With "SOLD" stamped on it.

He parked and got out, then yanked the sold sign stake out of the ground and tossed it down in the yard. "I'm never selling this house," he said, as he stormed up on the front porch and snatched open the screen door.

He barged inside.

"Tre Pound, in here."

The voice came from his living room. When he got there, he saw Carlo Masaccio sitting on his couch, alone, in an Italian suit with a silk pocket handkerchief. He looked stately and refined, even in a house as old as this. Mr. Masaccio clicked open his briefcase and told Tre Pound to have a seat.

"No," Tre Pound said.

"It's in your best interest to sit."

"I'm not signing my house over to nobody. I was born and raised in this house. This is my house, my 'hood, and I'm not leaving. So you might as well pack that shit up."

"Legally, this is not your house, Mr. King. It belongs to Shelton now. It's stipulated in WITSEC that you hand over all personal property prior to inclusion in the program. However, this paperwork I'm holding right now has nothing to do with this house. This isn't a real estate appointment."

"What kind of appointment is it?"

"It's an appointment with death."

Tre Pound heard someone behind him but didn't turn, not even when that someone put a gun to the side of his head.

"Who's behind me?" Tre Pound asked.

"It's a friend of yours," said Carlo. "Marlon Hayes. He so desperately wants to take your life but can't unless you let him. If you sign, you give him permission."

"Why would I be stupid enough to sign?"

"Because your reputation is spiraling down to irrelevancy, Mr. King. You cooperated with the FBI in securing a conviction against someone you've looked up to your whole life. You're currently in the witness protection program. You impregnated your 15-year-old cousin. The best thing you can do is die now before you make your reputation worse. Your uncle Cutthroat is still revered to this day. You can be revered too if you sign here. You wanted out the program, right? Here's your exit."

Wow, Tre Pound thought. *Carlo Masaccio really is about his business. He really is the best at what he does.*

Carlo held out a fancy pen. The tip looked wet. Blood red and wet, seconds away from dripping on the contract and ruining it.

Marlon Hayes lowered his gun and shoved Tre Pound forward.

Rolling up his sleeves, Tre Pound went and sat down next to Carlo, took the pen and turned to the back page. In neat and legible cursive, he spelled out "Levour" on the signature line, zipping through the v-o-u-r lightning fast but pausing at the "K" in his last name. He looked up at Marlon, who was holding the Glock at his side, clenching his jaw out-in-out-in and tapping his forefinger against the trigger guard in a rhythm, waiting as patiently as he could for the formalities to be over.

"The faster you sign," Carlo Masaccio said, "the faster you become a legend."

Tre Pound took a deep breath. He didn't want to be known as the gangster-turned-snitch who changed his life in the witness protection program. He was better than that. He was a King. If he was murdered now, at the hands of one of his homeboys, there could still be some prominence in his death and respect when people mentioned his name posthumously.

"It's not suicide," said the lawyer. "It's the only way out of the program."

"Sign it!" Marlon screamed.

Biting down on his bottom lip, Tre Pound took his eyes off an irate Marlon and stared back down at the contract. Only his last name was missing. He tapped the back of the pen against the sheet anxiously—*taptaptap*. He was still thinking, still undecided.

Taptaptap.

***

Tre Pound suddenly sat up in his twin bed and looked around the hotel room for Carlo Masaccio and Marlon. They weren't here anymore. They never were, he realized. He'd been dreaming.

With his hands he slowly smushed his face down, as if pulling his sweat-soaked skin would also remove the memories of the dream. It didn't. He could still feel Marlon hovering over him, waiting for him to sign.

Taptaptap.

The sound came from the bathroom ... where his money was stashed. Tre Pound threw the covers back and stood up. He pushed the bathroom door open so hard it smacked against the wall with a *bang*.

And startled Camille. "What the hell, Tre Pound? Damn, learn how to knock. You scared me, now I'm bleeding."

Camille had her right leg propped up on the sink. There was a prick of blood near her ankle where she'd been shaving. She swiped it with her thumb, sucked it, wiped her moist thumb on her gym shorts and pressed it against the baby cut.

"Can you hand me a Band-Aid?" she asked.

"Where are they?"

"I don't know. Check the cabinets."

He found one and opened it up for her, then let her put it on herself. He tried not to stare between her legs.

"I heard a noise," he said.

She tapped the razor against the sink a couple times to demonstrate. "That noise? I'm just trying to make my legs look beautiful."

"In the middle of the night?"

"I had a bad dream," she said. "I dreamed I was back in that parking garage with Dominique's dead body, and I'm trying to stay up so that the dream will pass out of my system. I'm hoping it works like that. It usually does. Just stay up until it passes."

"Only yo brain works like that."

"Shut up, Tre Pound."

Tediously, she brought the razor up her calf toward her knee in one long stroke. She put the blade under the faucet water, *taptaptapped* it, and started up the same leg, different path. Tre Pound didn't see the point. Her legs were already silky smooth. He watched her shave for a moment, and didn't notice how enthralled he was until she cut her eyes at him and smiled, flirty.

"Like my legs?"

"Just as much as I like road kill," he said.

"What are you doing up? You had a bad dream too?"

"I have bad dreams every night. I got a question for you though."

"Mm-hmm."

"Last night you asked me about having a son, something about having enemies and keeping him safe. Why did you ask me that?"

She pricked herself again, accidentally. "Dammit. Can you hand me another Band-Aid? This is bullcrap, and I don't even have any clean jeans to cover these cuts up."

"Why did you ask me about a son?"

"Can I not get a Band-Aid first and get this cleaned up?"

"Nah, answer the question."

"My question last night was just a question. I'm worried about your safety. I can't ask you questions no more? I'm not pregnant, if that's what you're thinking."

Tre Pound glared at her for a moment. "Yes, you are," he said, then pushed off the door frame and walked away.

"No, I'm not!"

Chapter 17

Camille had her comforter stuffed between her legs, as she laid curled up in the hotel twin bed. Her eyes had just fluttered open. Without even moving she could see Tre Pound's covers across from her, balled up and rumpled all over in a way that suggested he had a hard night. She lifted her head a little to see if he was still sleep.

He wasn't.

He was gone.

She pushed the sheets off her like they'd been evil to her, then swung her legs out of bed and looked around the room with her eyes half closed. Sitting there, she tried to remember which bag her print pants were in.

"Tre Pound, are you in the bathroom? I have to pee really really bad."

He didn't respond. And she didn't expect him to. He was Tre Pound—half ruffian, half selective-hearing ball of disrespect. She regretted mentioning pregnancy to him last night. She shouldn't have thrown that out there. She thought it would have been better to beat him to it, to mention it before he mentioned it because she knew "pregnant" was what he was thinking ... but now she wasn't so sure. Maybe she should have let him say it first. And then denied it. In hindsight, she wondered if it made her look guiltier. It probably did. Tre Pound was good at reading people.

I shouldn't have lied to him, she thought now. *He needs to know.*

She stood up and went to the bathroom, pushing it open without knocking like he did to her last night. "Tre, I have to—" But he wasn't in here. He wasn't in the hotel room at all. She rolled her shorts to her knees and sat down on the toilet. Something told her to look up. She did.

One of the ceiling tiles was pushed to the side.

After she flushed, she put the lid down and stood on top of it, where she was able to step onto the sink and feel inside the hole in the ceiling. The bag of money was missing.

Did he leave me here? Did he already go turn himself in?

Panicking, she darted out of the bathroom and out the door of the hotel room onto the tier overlooking the parking lot below. She didn't see Tre Pound's Infiniti M anywhere. Where his car had been parked last night, there was now a black Porsche Panamera in its place.

Did he really fucking leave me here? she thought again with more assurance that he did in fact abandon her—and their child. *I shouldn't have opened my mouth about me being pregnant. That bastard left me here stranded!* She shook the railing hard, tried to break it loose—it wobbled but didn't break—and she growled angrily.

"Fuck you, Tre Pound!" she screamed at the parking lot. She turned and went inside, slammed the door, grabbed her phone and dialed his number.

He answered. "Wussup?"

"Where the fuck did you go?! Did you fuckin' leave me?!"

"Yes, ma'am."

"You're a fucking coward, I swear," she cried. "What am I supposed to do? I don't have nobody to take care of me."

"What is wrong with you? I came back."

She paused. "You're not either back. Where's your car? Where's all the money?"

"I took the money to Buttercup's house. I didn't like keeping it in the room. It wasn't safe there, especially not in a one-way-in/one-way-out type of room. And then I got this cop murder warrant on my head. As far as my car ... the Infiniti, it's gone. You're the one who said you weren't riding in it no more, so I got another one. You didn't see my new Porsche?"

She smiled, wiping her tears. "Where are you?"

"I'm at the pool, smoking a blunt and getting my thoughts together before I turn myself in tomorrow."

"Can I join you?"

"No."

"I'm on my way."

***

It was an outdoor pool, but enclosed in the middle of the hotel complex, where people could stand outside their rooms and lean on their rails and watch guests swim.

Today, Tre Pound and Camille were the only two enjoying the clear, mirror blue water. Camille sat on the edge of the pool with her feet submerged. Underwater, her toes looked fishy white and blurred. Tre Pound was beside her but resting inside the pool, the cool water waving and eddying against his chest. He had his elbows resting out, back-of-the-couch style, as he took a tote of his blunt.

121

Camille looked around. There was an older white man in an ugly thriftstore-ish plaid shirt with lots of white facial hair watching them from one of the top tiers. He was smoking a cigarette, leaning on the rail. Just watching them, unabashedly. He looked harmless.

"Remember when you taught me how to swim at the Hard Rock Hotel and Café in Vegas?" Camille asked.

"Yeah. Family vacation."

"I wish we could go back to those times. When my momma was alive. Don't you ever wish you could go back?"

"I don't think like that. I'm not a fairytale-ass nigga. I live in the right-now."

Camille paddled her feet, but not enough to make a splash. "Where am I gonna go when you turn yourself in tomorrow?"

"With Buttercup," Tre Pound stated.

"No way, not in this lifetime. Ain't that the girl that stabbed you up? Me and her will not see eye to eye. I'll end up hurting her, I know I will."

"It's either Buttercup or begging Bernice to take you back. Your pick."

"Why can't I stay here, or get a suite?"

"A 15-year-old living out of a hotel? You won't last long. You need to be in somebody's house."

"You still trust her?"

"I do. She'll bend over backwards for me. She'll die for me. Most bitches I fuck wit' will."

Camille paddled some more, feeling awkward about what he just said. *Am I one of his bitches now that we've slept together? Did he see me that way? I'll die for him. Does that make me like the rest? But I would've died for him before we had sex.* She tried not to compare herself to his other females, but it was hard not to.

She pushed off the ledge and splashed into the pool in front of Tre Pound.

"What the hell are you doing?" he complained. "You got my blunt wet. You don't even have on swim clothes."

"That's because you went to go get yourself some swim shorts and didn't get me any. Selfish." Camille was treading water in a yellow t-shirt and the gym shorts she had on yesterday, her panties soaked underneath. "Race me."

"No, I'm smoking."

"If you love me, you'll race me."

"I guess I don't love you then."

Camille let the water pull her close to him. She'd seen the look in his eyes last night when she was shaving her legs. He wanted her. And there were other moments when she caught him glancing at her secretly, wantonly, whether he'd admit it or not. Even since she'd been sitting there poolside he had looked over at her legs nine times. She counted. She even let her feet brush up against his torso underwater, more than once—more than *twice*—and he didn't tell her to stop.

She decided to test him.

Playfully, she snatched the blunt from him and swam toward the middle of the pool one-handed, keeping the blunt high above water so it wouldn't get wet.

Tre Pound dove underwater and swam after her.

As she almost reached the other end of the pool, he caught her ankle and pulled her in. She let him, and when she was close enough she wrapped her legs around his waist underwater, wrapped her arms around his neck and pushed her lips into his forcefully. To her surprise, he didn't try to pull her off, at least not right away. When he did, she was still wrapped around him, staring in his eyes.

Was I wrong for kissing you? she asked him with her gaze.

He looked up at the white man.

Camille said, "He doesn't know you're my cousin."

"You just kissed me," Tre Pound said, his expression blank. "You wanna play, huh?"

"No, I'm tired of playing, Tre Pound. I'm serious right now. I know how you feel about me. Your dick is getting hard right now, I feel it. You can pretend and deny me all you want to but you're going against nature. Naturally, you love me. Naturally, I love you. Naturally, we're in love with each other. I've seen how you've been looking at me."

"Nah, I think you wanna play."

"Did you not just hear me?"

His eyes are changing, Camille suddenly noticed, dreading it, as the water eddied against their shoulders quietly. The water was almost musical, the moment was right, but Tre Pound was shutting her out, trying to suppress his true feelings for her. She could see it in his eyes. He was turning cold like he'd done before.

"Don't shut down on me," Camille pleaded. "Look at what's going on around us. Our family is falling apart. We need each other right now."

"You lied to me," he said.

"What?"

Camille creased her brow, giving him her clueless look. But inside she was screaming to herself, *This is your chance! Stop looking at him crazy. Tell him you're pregnant. He already knows.*

Yet, she just kept staring at him, too scared to come out with it. "What are you talking about, Tre Pound?"

"Yep. You still wanna play games."

"No, I don't. I—"

Tre Pound dunked her underwater. She pulled her legs from around his waist fast and tried to push off the bottom of the pool to shoot back up to the surface. He didn't let her. He held her down and she panicked, kicking and flailing her water-heavy legs and arms as if there was something she could grab onto. Just when she was about to take that mortal breath, he let her up.

She splashed through the surface, gasping for air. She started coughing violently. Her nose burned.

"Having fun yet?" he asked. Then to her horror he dunked her again.

He's trying to kill me!

This time, though, he didn't leave her down as long. When she broke through the surface again she pushed away from him and tried to catch her breath from a distance. Snatching the wet hair from out of her eyes, she saw him taking heavy steps toward her with the biggest grin, him wafting through the water with his chest.

"Stay away from me!" she screamed.

"I thought we were having fun."

Camille swam to the other end of the pool and immediately shoved herself out of the water dripping wet. Her shirt and shorts were drenched, weighing her down. But she still stalked away as fast as she could. The drips of water followed her.

"You owe me a blunt!" Tre Pound yelled.

Looking back over her shoulder in full fury, she flipped him off. Up above, still perched on the top tier, was the old white man holding the last of his cigarette close to his lips while smiling a set of missing teeth. He looked delighted by the show. Camille flipped him off too.

Chapter 18

Camille was blow-drying her hair in the mirror, using her hands to help ruffle it and billow so it would dry faster. She had already rung out her shirt and shorts and let them hang over the lip of the sink. She had on a dry pair of boy shorts and a sports bra.

For some reason she felt naked when Tre Pound entered the room and shut the door behind him. Her heart started beating faster, as she watched him in the mirror walking up behind her. He had a drying towel draped over his shoulder. She kept blow-drying, trying to pretend he wasn't here.

"Are you done playing?" he asked.

She ignored him. She wasn't as angry as she was when she first got out the pool but she was still mad. She'd thought he had tried to kill her, but after thinking about it she realized if he had wanted to, he could have. Still, she didn't like being played with like that.

She wondered if that was his point. *Did he play with my life in the pool because I was playing with the life of his child by not telling him it existed?* She didn't know, and she didn't feel like trying to figure him out.

Tre Pound took the blow-dryer from her gently and shut it off. So she picked up her comb and started running it through her kinky hair as if nothing had just happened. But then the comb started getting stuck; she needed the blow-dryer.

Ragefully, she slammed the comb down and turned on her heels to face him. "I'm pregnant!" she yelled at him. "Okay? There, I said it. I'm pregnant. Now you know."

"Why are you just now telling me?"

"Because I was waiting for the right moment, when our lives weren't moving so fast."

"Don't ever lie to me about something like that. You hear me?"

"Yes."

Camille felt relief. He didn't look upset that she was carrying his child. He went and sat down on the edge of the bed and she joined him. She picked up his hand and set it on her thigh, then her hand on top of his—a gesture of togetherness—but he pulled away and laid flat on the bed. Camille sighed.

"How did you know I was pregnant?" she asked.

"I've been around enough women to know when one's pregnant. I had suspicions for a while but when you asked me about a son yesterday, that made it real. Then as I was watching you shave in the bathroom, I smelled vomit. You didn't clean it up good enough. Then you just flat-out came out and said you *weren't* pregnant, which was pretty much you're way of saying you were."

"I'm sorry for lying."

"Yeah, whatever. Let's just be glad we caught it while it can still be reversed."

She looked at him as if he'd lost his mind. He said it so insensitively, like their child was a disease. *Glad we caught it,* he'd said. Cleary, they were on two different pages.

"You don't wanna keep the baby?" she asked.

He fake laughed. "Hell nah."

"I do."

"I bet you do. That's how yo young mind works. You don't think about the consequences. That's why I made the decision for us."

"It's my body. And I'm keeping it."

Tre Pound sat up and stared at her, face to face. "No you're not, Camille."

Her lips were tight as she stared back, defiant.

"You're not having that baby," he said. "I put that on my dead homie Stacks you're not. If you don't do it willingly, I'ma make it happen."

Camille knew what he was saying. It gave her the chills. "You'll kill me?" she asked.

"If I have to, I will."

"Me? You'll kill me? You promised my daddy you would take care of me and now you're talking about you're gonna kill me? And your child? I know you're not that heartless. I know you're not."

"Here's how I been looking at it the last few hours," he began. "If yo body gets to the stage where you can't have an abortion, you're saying fuck me. You know how I'll look in the streets if it got out that you're carrying my seed? My reputation, all the work I put in, will be overshadowed by that. So if you try to ruin me in that way then that means you're really against me." He paused to let his words sink in. "That's how I'ma justify killing you in my head. I'll be able to sleep at night."

"Your reputation is more important than me?"

"Yes."

"People don't even have to know the baby is yours. I've been tellin' people it's Jesse's."

He cocked his head. "Telling' who?"

"I only told Krystal. People will believe that it's Jesse's baby."

"They won't have to believe anything because the baby is disappearing."

"We can leave Kansas City, Tre Pound. What the fuck is here? Nothing but drama. We can start over in a new city. Me and you."

He rubbed his forehead, jaded. Then he suddenly slapped his hand down on the mattress and startled her. "There is no me and you, Camille! Don't start that shit back up. You're acting like Dominique."

Camille shot to her feet and went over and climbed in her bed, angrily snatched the sheets up to her chest. He just compared her to Dominique, and that had her fiery hot. She stared at the ceiling, trying not to cry. *He does look at me like just another one of his bitches,* she thought.

Tre Pound looked over at her. She didn't give him the pleasure of eye contact. He tossed the remote control on her bed. "Turn the TV on and take yo mind off that shit. I'm getting in the shower. In a few hours we're heading over to Buttercup's. A'ight?"

Camille turned away from him and pulled the covers over her head.

***

"How do you like it?" Tre Pound asked Camille, as he pushed the Porsche down Troost Avenue an mph above speed limit.

"Like what?" she asked, grumpy.

"The new ride?"

She shrugged.

"You still mad, huh?"

"I'm fine," she lied.

They had just come from Go Chicken Go to grab a box of Tre Pound's favorite gizzards and now they were heading to Buttercup's house. The box was in his lap, and he was eating from it one gizzard at a time, licking his fingers, not sharing with her. Camille had told him she wasn't hungry when they were in drive-thru. She was so upset she didn't want to eat.

She still couldn't get over what he asked her to do—and the callous way in which he asked her to do it. It was like standard procedure to him. *Glad we caught it.* She, on the other hand, saw the baby inside her as a new beginning, a new source of love in her world, a love that wouldn't turn its back on her like people in the past had. Like Tre Pound was starting to again. Camille knew that the *mother-child* love was eternal. It was what she needed, what she'd been longing for. She couldn't see herself going through with the abortion and coming out with her sanity.

"We're here," said Tre Pound, as he parked and pulled up the emergency break.

Camille gathered her luggage out the trunk, every piece of it, slinging the backpack over her shoulder and hobbling up to the front door awkwardly because her stuff was heavy. Tre Pound walked just ahead of her with his own backpack on; everything he needed had fit inside of it. Camille grew angrier each step she took, mad that he didn't help her carry anything. She was still pregnant, after all.

Tre Pound knocked. "Behave," he said to Camille.

Buttercup opened the door and smiled, immediately hugging Tre Pound. "Hey, baby." Then she looked at

Camille. "Your little cousin is cute." She extended her hand. "I'm Buttercup."

Camille had to set a suitcase down to shake her hand. She really didn't want to, but she did.

Buttercup was a beautiful girl. Camille could admit that. She could see what Tre Pound saw in her. Buttercup was curvy, way more curves than Camille for sure. Buttercup stood with her hands in the back pockets of her jeans after she let them in, sort of letting Camille look the place over, and all Camille could think was, *Wow, she has big titties. Dominique had big titties too. Is that the type of girls Tre Pound likes? Buttercup doesn't look that much older than me.*

"My home is your home," Buttercup said to Camille.

"No it's not," Camille replied.

Buttercup smiled again, dutifully, like a waitress. "She's cute."

"Where can she put her stuff?" Tre Pound asked.

"I have a room ready for her. Right this way, ladies and gentlemen."

The room where Camille was assigned to was smaller than the one she had at Bernice's. It would be the smallest room she ever slept in. If two people stood side by side and stretched their arms out, they would be able to touch the east and west walls easily. It was closet-sized. They had passed a room bigger than this one a door down.

"What's wrong with that other room?" Camille asked. "The one next door that we just passed."

"That's my work-out room," Buttercup explained. "If you need anything, just holler. Me and your cousin will be right across the hall."

Camille set her luggage down by the bed, as Buttercup shut the door on her way out. Camille went to the door and opened it back up slightly so she could peek through the crack. She saw Tre Pound grab a handful of Buttercup's booty, as they scampered in the room across the hall.

Two love birds.

Buttercup turned to close their door and looked surprised to see Camille watching them through the crack. Camille shot her a glare that said, *That's supposed to be me in there with Tre Pound, you bitch.* It was as if Buttercup read her mind, because she smiled at Camille teasingly— then slammed the door shut.

Chapter 19

In the parking garage of a 12-story building in downtown Kansas City, Tre Pound stepped out of his Porsche in a white V-neck tee and sweatpants, with new patent leather Air Jordans on his feet. He grabbed the duffel bag of money out the trunk and slung the strap on his shoulder. Locking his ride with the remote, he stuffed the keys in his sweats and strolled across the garage to the elevator.

He felt optimistic. He was going to pay Carlo Masaccio his retainer, turn himself in, bond out the same day—just like he did on his last murder case—and then he was going to head back home and fuck the shit out of Buttercup. In the days to come, he had a lot to do. First, he had to get Camille in the abortion clinic. Then he had to kill Marlon, try to draw him out in the open somehow. Then and only then would Tre Pound feel safe enough to reclaim his house on 35th Street. Niggas had tried to run him out of his 'hood before but ...

It would never happen.

Stepping off the elevator, Tre Pound knew right where he needed to go. He stopped at the secretary's desk and put the duffelbag on the counter.

"Is that for me?" asked Rose, who'd been Carlo Masaccio's right-hand girl since the King family had been using this firm. She smiled and poked the bag with her pen.

"It sure is for you," Tre Pound replied, "if you can beat this double-murder I got."

"Oh, darn. That sounds like a job for my boss. Have you talked to him yet? Did you set up an appointment?"

"No, ma'am, I didn't. He usually just tells me to come on in if I have an issue. We don't talk on the phone much."

"Well, things are changing around here. Appointments are mandatory now. He's been real busy with a new case."

Shelton's case, Tre Pound knew.

"Do I need to come back later, after I set up an appointment? I don't mind. I really don't wanna turn myself in today anyway. I was just trying to get it over with."

"Well, no, just have a seat while I try to get him on the line. You're one of his biggest clients, and I don't want him to get mad at me for sending you home."

Tre Pound had a seat, placing the duffel bag on the floor at his feet. He pulled his car keys out just to look at the Porsche emblem on the key fob. He wondered if the remote start would work from ten floors up.

"He's ready for you," said Rose.

Tre Pound got up with his bag and headed to Carlo Masaccio's office. When he walked in, Carlo was sitting at his desk scribbling on sticky notes and attaching them to files scattered on his desk. Tre Pound had never seen his work area this cluttered.

"Got time for me?" Tre Pound asked, having a seat. "I got a lot of money for you if you do."

Carlo snatched his glasses off and stood up to shake Tre Pound's hand. "I'm sorry, I'm just so busy with your cousin's federal case."

"How's it going?"

"I'm afraid I can't reveal that information."

"That's fine. I need to get this cop murder shit taken care of."

"I saw your face on the news. They picked a bad photo of you. I almost didn't recognize you."

"They always do that to me. This should be an open and shut case, though. I'm the one who called the police to my house. I reported the break-in, so how am I a suspect? I'm thinking once I turn myself in, they'll turn around and let me right back out—for sure, if you're with me."

"Mr. King, I can't represent you."

Tre Pound blinked. "Come again?"

"I can't be your attorney any more. It's a conflict of interest in my current case with Shelton King."

"I don't have nothing to do with his case."

"That's just not true, Levour." Carlo leaned forward, elbows on his desk and fingers intertwined. "You're a big part of his case."

"In what way?"

"I can't discuss."

"Did Shelton tell you not to represent me no more?"

"Levour, I'm sorry but I have a lot of work to do. I can refer you to another attorney that has high credentials outside of my firm. If your case is as open and shut as you say, you won't have a problem."

Carlo scribbled the information down on a sticky note and handed it to Tre Pound, who took a second to read the name—Miron Schnoll—before folding the note so the adhesive would stick to itself. He put it in his pocket.

"I wish you the best of luck," said Carlo.

***

Miron Schnoll was at retirement age. His skin was thin and wrinkly and his knuckles were spotted with some type of skin disease. Tre Pound cringed when he shook his hand; it was rubbery.

"Miron Schnoll. Nice to meet you."

"Levour King. Nice to meet you too."

Tre Pound had a seat in his office and told him what he knew about his case, that two Kansas City police officers had been killed in his home and that he was innocent, which should be easy to prove considering that his phone records would show that he was nowhere near his house when he reported the break-in. He left out his knowledge of Marlon committing the crime and that Cash and Seneca were in the house when the shooting took place. That information would be left for detectives to figure out on their own. Tre Pound had his bases covered.

But Mr. Miron Schnoll wanted to play devil's advocate. "Until all the facts come out, you need to be prepared for this to go to trial," he said. "Two cops were killed, and I guarantee you that the city will want justice regardless of who's actually guilty. And right now the media reports I've seen say you're the only suspect. They're gonna play hard ball. They're gonna want a conviction, a hefty one."

Tre Pound crossed his arms. Carlo Masaccio never gave worst case scenarios.

Together, they left the office and rode in Miron's Lincoln Towncar down to the station. Miron looked like an old chauffeur in his black suit, not an experienced lawyer. They talked fees on the way there, base payments and hypothetical situations—like the hiring of investigators—

that could become costly if the prosecution turned out to have a strong case.

"You're cheaper than Carlo Masaccio," Tre Pound said. "Why is that?"

"Uh ... I'm not sure. I charge what I think is fair."

"You're just as good as him, though, right?"

"Absolutely. I'm the best."

A moment later Miron and Tre Pound were walking down the sidewalk toward the station. Miron held the door open for him and let him go in first. There was a brief wait as the officer at the counter searched for Tre Pound's profile. It was clear she found it when her forehead creased in concern.

"Your Levour King?" said the female officer. She looked back at her computer, then up again, obviously comparing images.

"I look meaner in my pictures," Tre Pound explained.

"He's turning himself in today," said Miron. "And we're prepared to make bond today also."

"He doesn't have a bond."

Tre Pound's heart started beating faster.

"He should," Miron said. "I called down here and confirmed his case number and bond amount. It should be one million, ten percent through the courts."

"On his murder warrant there is a one million dollar bond," she said, pointing to her screen as if they could see it. "But on this other one"—she was squinting at the monitor now—"there is no bond."

"What other one?" Tre Pound asked.

"You have another warrant for rape," she said.

Chapter 20

"What's your name?"

"Levour King."

"Do you have any aliases?"

"Yes."

"And they are?"

"Just one. Tre Pound."

As Ms. Trisha Booker typed in his information, Tre Pound looked to the right of him. There was a line of inmates in orange jumpsuits waiting to sit in his seat and be processed. It looked like they were upset that he was taking so long, as if he had any control over how long it took. *What the fuck are yall looking at?* he said to them with his eyes.

Ms. Trisha Booker was a medium build, late-thirtyish-looking woman. Her hair was long and fresh, with end-curls that seemed to bounce off the shoulders of her uniform. It was a hairstyle that would've looked better on a more attractive girl.

"Mr. King, it seems that you're a popular man here at the Jackson County Detention Center," said Ms. Booker. "A lot of people have you listed as an enemy."

"How's that? I haven't been in the county in I don't know how long."

"During the intake process, which is what we're going through now, I ask every inmate if they have enemies. Not just incarcerated enemies, but enemies anywhere. Enemies happen to end up in here together all the time. Our job is to keep them away from each other. Do you have any?"

Tre Pound could name enemies for days—Marlon, Hoodey, Shelton, Spook, the whole 12th Street neighborhood, even a few females. And then there were enemies he didn't know by name, some not even by face. He had robbed a lot of people in Kansas City.

"I have enemies galore," Tre Pound said, "but I don't wanna list any."

"That's fine," Ms. Booker said. "Are you in a gang."

"No."

"What neighborhood are you from?"

"Tre block."

"That sounds like a gang."

"It's just a neighborhood."

Booker typed the information in anyway. She looked surprised by the results. "From what my computer says, individuals from Tre block, or 35th Street, are known for crimes against other neighborhoods. Such as robbery, theft, murder, and extortion. Known enemies are—gosh, there's a lot—43rd Street, 72nd Street, 23rd Street, 10th Street, 51st Street, 27th Street, 67th Street, and 12th Street. There's actually an asterisk beside 12th Street." She searched her screen for the meaning behind the asterisk. "Okay, here it is, and I quote, 'All persons from geo-area 35th Street are NOT to be put in the same wing as any member from geo-area 12th Street. Absolutely NO exceptions.'"

140

"It says all that in there?" Tre Pound asked. He was surprised by how accurate it was.

"Right here in black and white. We screen every inmate that comes through our doors, thousands upon thousands, and we gather information from these guys and start to build a database. Knowing the different gang affiliations, the neighborhoods, the beefs—or funk I think it's called here, sorry I'm from Minnesota—it all helps us keep inmates alive. So that means, with the information you provided, if we can't find you a wing where you don't have enemies, then we might have to put you in protective custody."

"I'm not doing PC. I'm Tre Pound. I'm a King. We don't do protective custody. Does it say that on yo little computer?"

"It does not," Booker said. "But if you refuse PC, then we'll have to place you in administrative segregation."

"I don't care. Anything but PC."

Ms. Booker worked her magic, exploring the system with experienced fingers against her keyboard. Tapping, squinting at the monitor, shaking her head no, tapping some more. Tre Pound waited patiently, one of the only inmates in orange who was.

Then Booker looked at Tre Pound with a raised eyebrow. A sign that she was about to give him an ultimatum. " I'll tell you what ..." she began. "I have a module where no one has you listed as an enemy. But it's on the 4th floor."

"I'll take it," Tre Pound said.

"I have to warn you, though. Inmates on the 4th floor are territorial. Most, if not all, have been to prison a time or two, or they've been sitting here in county for a while and have developed short tempers. I don't normally start new inmates off on the 4th floor. It's dangerous."

"I'll be alright," Tre Pound told her. "I can handle my own."

***

The door to module 4-A buzzed open slowly, as Tre Pound stood in front of it waiting for it to open. Inmates on the other side were watching him, waiting to see what new arrival was entering their space.

"We got a young nigga," someone called out, as the door came to a stop.

Tre Pound stepped inside the wing, not caring who made the comment. He carried a cardboard box filled with the basics—sheets, pillow, toothpaste, toothbrush, soap, and two tiny clear bottles that Trisha swore were toothpaste and shampoo. As he headed to his cell, he made eye contact with the inmates who were staring at him. No fear. Other inmates were going about their business, either on the phone or playing cards or watching TV.

Tre Pound ducked inside his cell and dropped his box on the bed.

This was home.

"Tre Pound?"

Instincts caused Tre Pound to pivot toward the voice, and his right elbow twitched in preparation to throw a punch. Standing at his door was a guy he recognized. A shorter guy, light-skinned, skinny, wavy hair. It was Lil' Pat, Camille's coward ex-boyfriend.

He walked inside the cell, smiling. "Wussup, Tre Pound? I thought that was you. I'm Lil' Pat, Hoodey's little brother. I used to talk to yo cousin—"

Tre Pound punched him. Perfect hook to the jaw. Lil' Pat fell in the corner, holding his face. There was immediate commotion outside the cell. Inmates stirring, looking in. Tre Pound waited for someone else to run in and help.

And one did.

An inmate with his jumper rolled down around his waist appeared. He was wearing a white tee that hung over his waist, where the arms of the orange jumper were tied in a knot. His fists were balled.

This mystery inmate looked down at Lil' Pat, then up at Tre Pound. Then he stepped inside the cell at a threatening pace.

"Hold up," said Lil Pat.

The inmate paused.

Tre Pound said, "Nah, keep it coming'. I got something for you too."

"No, it's cool. Kenneth, he's cool," Lil' Pat said, standing back up. "This is Tre Pound."

Kenneth looked Tre Pound over. "So what? Didn't this nigga just hit you?"

"Nah, he didn't hit me. You didn't hit me, did you, Tre Pound?"

Tre Pound was trying to figure out what was going on. When did Lil' Pat have goons? This inmate ready to fight Tre Pound looked like a 'hood nigga—tats on his neck, muscles bulging through his shirt, gold tooth. This was someone Lil' Pat would run from, not command.

"Right, Tre Pound?" Lil' Pat asked again. "You didn't hit me, did you?" He had a nervous expression on his face. *Go along with it*, he was saying.

Tre Pound read him. But didn't care. "Yeah, I hit you. I should've hit you harder."

Kenneth lurched forward but Lil' Pat got in his way, holding him back. Lil' Pat managed to push him out the cell, and with Kenneth being of a larger build than Lil Pat he could've easily shoved Lil' Pat to the side. But he let the kid push him out.

He doesn't really wanna fight me, Tre Pound knew. *He must know I'm a King.*

Lil' Pat pulled the cell door near closed, giving him and Tre Pound privacy from Kenneth, who was pacing outside the cell.

"He's overprotective," Lil' Pat said.

"That's gay," Tre Pound replied.

"My brother Hoodey hired him to look out for me while I'm in here."

"Yo brother is gay too."

Lil' Pat frowned, then leaned against the wall with his knee bent, giving Tre Pound his space. "We're on the same team, Tre Pound. Didn't you hear that my brother gave yo cousin Shelton a million dollars to get him out of jail?"

"He didn't 'give' him shit. It was a loan. Kings don't take hand-outs."

"He still helped him out. Shelton's out, ain't he?"

Tre Pound ignored the question. "I'm not your homie, you're not my friend, we're not on the same team, none of that shit. You killed a nigga in front of Camille, my baby cousin. If she would've got hurt, I would've locked that door behind you and made you touch every wall in this room. I would've let Kenneth watch."

"I really care about Camille, Tre Pound. She was never in harm's way."

"She was close enough to get blood splatter on her face."

"I'm sorry, Tre Pound."

"Sorry yo way on out my cell."

Lil' Pat was hesitant to leave. He still had something on his mind, questions in his eyes. "I wanted to know if you'd call Camille so I can talk to her. My brother helped yall out so I was wondering if I could get that favor. Please? At least so I can apologize to her."

Tre Pound pointed toward the door. "If you don't get the fuck out my cell, I'ma kill you."

Lil' Pat sucked his teeth, then finally left.

Tre Pound made his bed and sat down on it. He leaned on his elbows, clasping his hands together at his lips in deep thought. He was trying to figure out how he got here. *What technology did the police use to determine that it was Camille, an underage girl, on the recording? Did they have audio and video? Did Shelton tell them it was Camille? Did he set me up? Did Carlo Masaccio refer me to Miron Schnoll to deliberately get me slapped with jail time?*

Tre Pound started biting his thumbnail. He didn't know if his thoughts held any real weight ... or if he was just paranoid.

Chapter 21

Camille felt an instant rush of pure joy when the knob to Buttercup's room turned when she twisted it, surprised that it wasn't locked. She pushed the door wide, let it swing all the way open and bump the dresser behind it. It started to swing back, but Camille stepped inside the room before it did.

The door closed shut on its own.

The initial triumph she felt when she busted in here seemed to wither the more steps she took. Her joy was replaced by a throbbing sense of unease. She knew Buttercup had to be still at work—for at least another couple hours to make a full eight-hour day—but there was that imaginative part of her brain that pictured Buttercup springing out the closet shutters with a bowie knife screaming, *Get out my room you bitch aaargh!* It was silly, but Camille's heart was still pumping doubletime.

She opened the shutters.

Nobody popped out.

She went through Buttercup's clothes one hanger at a time, then unhooked one of the more daring outfits—a green one-shoulder bodycon dress. She turned it over; it had cut-outs for skin exposure running up the back of both legs. *Is this what Tre Pound likes his women to wear?* Camille wondered.

She put it back, went to the master bathroom and opened the medicine cabinet. She plucked a few prescription bottles off the shelf and read the labels. Aspirin on one, ibuprofen on another, sinus and congestion, Ambien Oral. There was nothing fancy here. And that was upsetting because Camille expected to see a bunch of crazy people medicine piled up. It would have proven her theory that sane people didn't stab people they love in the hand, then turn around and call the police on themselves like Buttercup did. Sane people knew when to just let a man go that didn't love them back. Right?

But maybe Camille was wrong. Maybe Buttercup really loved Tre Pound and was momentarily filled with so much rage over him replacing her that she attacked him. Maybe Buttercup was just in love.

Like me, Camille thought.

She put the bottles back in the cabinet then closed the mirror, and that's when she saw Buttercup's reflection standing behind her. Her squeal got caught in her throat.

"She's in my room snooping around," Buttercup said into the phone she was holding up to her ear, as she cut her eyes away from Camille and walked back out of the bathroom.

Camille followed her.

Buttercup was wearing her burgundy polo-style work shirt. Half of it was untucked. She suddenly turned around on a dime, startling Camille again, and fixed her with a glare.

"You wanna talk to her?" Buttercup asked the person she was talking to on the phone. "Okay ... hold on, here she is." She handed the cell phone to Camille.

Camille put it up to her ear on her way out the room. "Hello?"

"What are you doing in her room?" Tre Pound asked.

"I was just looking around. I don't know her. So I was investigating."

"That's not your business to be in her shit. Stay out of her room, okay?"

"Okay, I will. Where are you? You should've been back by now."

"I'm locked up."

The angst Camille felt was physical. "What happened? You gave the lawyer the bond money, didn't you?"

"Yeah, I submitted a bond on the murders but they had another charge on file that I can't bond out on yet."

"What charge?"

"That's not important right now."

Camille frowned. She looked at Buttercup, who was standing in earshot. "Did you tell Buttercup what the charge is?"

"No. It's not her business either."

Camille believed him. "What do I need to do? Tell me."

"Has any FBI agents came to talk to you?" he asked.

"No. Why?"

"Any type of law enforcement whatsoever? Tell me the truth."

"Nobody talked to me, Tre Pound. Are they supposed to?"

"I don't know."

Camille sucked her teeth. "Well, if the police come at me, I'll tell you."

"A'ight. You know what to say if they do, right?"

"Yes. I'm not gonna say shit."

"That's what I like to hear. I'll call again soon when I got time. A'ight? Bye."

When the line went dead it made Camille flinch. He hung up too soon. She had more questions she wanted to ask.

"Phone, please," said Buttercup, with her palm out. Camille gave the cell phone a short underhanded toss, made her catch it. Buttercup almost dropped it, just barely saved it by pinning it against her thigh. "Softball my freshman and junior year," she said proudly. "Do you play sports?"

"I read."

"Me too," Buttercup smiled. "I also write. But you need some athleticism in your life. You should try volleyball or soccer next year. It's not as tough as softball. Sports will thicken you up."

Camille was thinking, *Bitch don't be giving me advice. You ain't that much older than me.*

"Tre Pound made me take a half day so I can run this extra money up to his lawyer for his new case," Buttercup said. "I should be back in a couple hours. Can I trust you not to go in my room again? Or do I need to lock it?"

Camille said, "I'd lock it if I was you."

Chapter 22

It took a few days for Tre Pound to learn how the inmates in this wing operated. From his seat in one of the plastic chairs pushed against the wall where he could overlook the whole module, he'd learned a lot. Some inmates just wanted to sit in front of the TV and watch the news or sitcoms. Pick their nose, ball it up and flick it, stare at the screen—that's it. A couple others gambled food trays all day in dice games, Monopoly, poker, spades, or any game they could think of. Kenneth was one of the gamblers. He was currently playing chess with a parole violator who wore a T-shirt tied around his head as a du-rag. The du-rag guy was winning, ahead on pieces and strategic position. Kenneth was scratching his chin in confusion.

To Tre Pound's right were the phones, and you could always catch Lil' Pat on one of them. Tre Pound thought he'd seen Lil' Pat crying one time, but when Pat saw Tre Pound staring quizzically at him, he lowered his head, burying it—as well as the phone—in his forearm to hide his face and talk in whispers.

These inmates are fascinating, Tre Pound thought, smiling to himself. *Weak, but fascinating.* He pulled his leg up on his lap and continued watching his surroundings comfortably.

"Tre Pound, telephone."

Tre Pound turned to see Lil' Pat holding the phone out to him.

"Who is it?" Tre Pound asked.

"My brother. Hoodey."

Tre Pound scooted his chair close and took the phone. "Hello?"

"Where's my money at?" Hoodey asked.

Tre Pound pulled the phone away from his ear, looking at the receiver, disgusted. *Who the fuck does Hoodey think he's talking to?*

Tre Pound handed the phone back to Lil' Pat. "Tell yo brother to come at me correct if he wants to talk to me," he said, scooting back to his look-out post.

A few seconds later Lil' Pat was asking Tre Pound to take the phone again. He snatched it, and spoke before Hoodey did.

"I'm not one of yo customers," Tre Pound said into the speaker, "and I never will be. Address me with your best foot forward, all manners, no bullshit. You hear me, you purple-lipped punk."

Hoodey chuckled. "I was just fucking wit' you, Tre Pound. I know you don't have my money. Stop being so sensitive."

"Yo momma's sensitive."

"I talked to Shelton. He told me what happened to the money."

"What did he say happened?"

"He said yo people got robbed and murdered. You haven't heard about Cash and Gutta?"

"Nah, I been in here."

"It happened before you got in there, bro-bro. Yo cousin's Gutta and Cash got smoked, and whoever did it took my money. I hate to be the one to break it to you but that's what it is. Shelton said he'll reimburse me, that's all I care about."

"He didn't tell you who he thinks did it?"

"Nope. He just said he knows it's somebody close."

"That's the words he used? *Somebody close?*"

"His exact words."

Shelton knew that Tre Pound killed Gutta and Cash and kept the money. But he didn't tell Hoodey, probably didn't tell anybody. That meant that Shelton was trying to keep this family falling-out on the hush. He didn't want outsiders to know how messy the King family was getting.

"If you know what happened to yo money," Tre Pound said to Hoodey, "then why did you need to talk to me?"

"I didn't. I just like fuckin' wit'cho tough ass and I wanted to rub it in yo face that you're locked up and I'm free. Also, I wanted to ask you why'd you kill them cops. I seen that shit on the news. You got the whole city hot as a muthafucka, making it hard for niggas like me to eat."

"I didn't kill no cops, you funny-looking nigga. But I'm glad it's harder for you to eat out there though."

"All bullshit aside, I need a favor from you. I need you to look out for my little brother while he's in there. I need you to make a call for him too. He wants to talk to your cousin Camille too. Just one phone call."

"Fuck you. I'm not your flunky. That's what you got Kenneth for."

Tre Pound gave Lil' Pat the phone back. He was turning to take his seat when he saw someone trying to get his attention in the wing across the hall. There was soundproof glass separating them so he couldn't hear the guy—but he did recognize him.

152

His name was Tommy. Hard to miss a short, pudgy, middle-aged man amongst a module full of younger fellas. Tommy was a renowned bank robber, an OG. He and his brother Tony had been robbing banks since—

It suddenly dawned on Tre Pound why Tommy was trying to get his attention. Not too long ago he'd caught Tony at the gas station. Tony said he had just escaped from the county jail—*from here*—and he accused Gutta of snitching on him and his brother Tommy during a jewelry store robbery. At the time Tre Pound thought he was lying, so he beat him up right there in front of the store, but while laying on his back Tony got the upperhand and started shooting at Tre Pound and would have killed him if Camille hadn't rammed the Infiniti into Tony, smashing him in between the hood and the bumper of another parked car. And after that, Tre Pound shot Tony in the head. He and Camille drove away that day and left Tony's body laying in the middle of the parking lot.

Now, Tre Pound was looking through the glass at an obviously angry Tommy, who was yelling words that Tre Pound couldn't hear. Tre Pound cuffed a hand behind his ear—*I can't hear you, nigga.*

Tommy started doing sign language. But Tre Pound didn't know how to read it.

"Anybody in here know sign language?" Tre Pound asked, turned to his wing-mates.

Almost the whole wing did, but Kenneth was the first to come over.

"See what this nigga is talking about for me," Tre Pound said.

Kenneth read Tommy's fingers. "He said you paralyzed his brother Tony."

He's alive?

"Tell him he shouldn't have shot at me," Tre Pound said.

Kenneth sent the message with hand signals. Tommy looked like he didn't like the response, so he sent another message, a lengthy one. Tommy was twisting his fingers all sorts of ways—hurriedly, it seemed—and Tre Pound wasn't sure if Kenneth could follow it all. But he could.

Kenneth said, "He said yo cousin Gutta snitched on him and you protected a snitch. He said you got Tony back locked up that day, he's in the medical wing downstairs and might not walk again. If it wasn't for you and Gutta, him and his brother would be free."

Back when that happened at the gas station, Tre Pound didn't know he was taking up for a snitch. He didn't know Gutta was a confidential informant.

Tre Pound shrugged. "Tell him Gutta is dead."

Kenneth hand-signaled it, eighteen quick finger motions. Then Tommy replied.

"He doesn't care that Gutta is dead," Kenneth explained. "He says you have to pay too. You have a $100,000 price on yo head from them 12th Street niggas and he's upping it to $200,000."

Tre Pound looked through the glass at Tommy, shrugging again. *Money on my head don't mean shit in here,* he thought. Then Tommy sent another message, a universal sign of death—he took his thumb and slowly swiped it across his own neck.

"You know what that means, don't you?" Kenneth asked.

"Yeah," Tre Pound replied. "He's gonna slit my throat. I'm shaking in my boots. Fuck that old-ass nigga."

Chapter 23

The next morning Tre Pound was sliding his feet into his orange rubber shower sandals, thinking about how he was going to handle Camille and that baby when he got out of here. He carried those thoughts with him to the showers, and as he soaped himself—scrubbing his armpits, lathering his chest and ballsack—he came to the conclusion that Camille would make the abortion happen on her own, without him breathing down her neck. She was a smart girl.

He had told her he would kill her if she didn't, but Camille had looked like she didn't believe him. Hell, Tre Pound didn't even believe himself when he said it. He couldn't kill Camille, could he? If he had it in him to put a bullet in Camille he would've did it the moment after they slept together. He had just been trying to scare her.

He stood under the water, closed his eyes and let his body rinse. *She'll get the abortion,* he assured himself.

A moment later he was dressed in orange and picking up the phone to call her.

She answered. "Hello?"

"Wussup, Camille?"

"Tre Pound, when are you coming home? I can't stand this bitch Buttercup."

"What's going on over there?"

"She's treating me like a child. She wants me to do dishes, sweep, trying to teach me how to vacuum like I don't already know how. I haven't even been here three days."

"Speaking of children ... have you looked into where you need to go to have that done?"

She paused. "I haven't. No."

"Get on top of that. Have Buttercup help you out."

"I thought you didn't want anybody else to know I was pregnant."

"She doesn't have to know. Just bring it up in casual conversation. Tell her you're asking for a friend. The bitch is dumb."

"When are you getting out?"

"Soon. The legal team is on it."

"Are you okay in there?"

"I'm Tre Pound. I'm okay everywhere."

There was a loud beeping over the intercom that got the whole module's attention. An announcement followed: "Levour King, report to the front of the module, fully dressed, immediately. Repeat: Levour King, report to the front of the module immediately."

Tre Pound looked to his left, where he could peer out the window down the hallway; he saw a guard coming. "Camille, I have to go. They're calling me somewhere."

"Okay. Be safe. I love you."

"I love you too."

"So you say ..." she added.

Tre Pound hung up, then stood at the front of the wing and waited for the guard to open the door. Something felt weird, something inside him that told him to turn around.

He looked over his shoulder.

Kenneth was staring at him. He was standing against the rail with a deck of cards in his hands, shuffling them idly. Just staring blankly, and shuffling. Earlier this morning during breakfast Lil' Pat told Tre Pound that Kenneth had been pulled out to go to court. He was back now, and apparently he'd been hit with a sentence that wasn't to his liking. He hadn't spoken to anybody since he returned, not even Lil' Pat.

"How much time did you get?" Tre Pound asked him.

Kenneth stopped shuffling and mugged him. "They gave me a life sentence."

"Ouch." Tre Pound turned back around. *Sucks to be you,* he thought.

***

"Where am I going?" Tre Pound asked the guard that was escorting him.

"You have a visit," he replied.

"My lawyer?"

"Nope. Detectives."

Fuck!

Tre Pound knew it was only a matter of time before he had a visit from the law. There was no preparing for it, no lessening the anxiety he felt. He entered the room with the two detectives who rose to their feet in comely suits. They introduced themselves as Detectives Bernard and Aurora. Bernard extended his hand for a shake.

Tre Pound looked at the hand as if it was contagious, then shook his head no. He stood by the seat he was supposed to sit in. "If I would've known ahead of time that yall was coming, I would've saved yall the trip. I'm not talking about nothing pertaining to nothing."

"Why don't you just have a seat for us, Mr. King," said Aurora.

"I'm fine standing."

Bernard sat down, then Aurora did. Aurora sighed, then said, "You're facing a lot of time, Mr. King. And you're starting off on the wrong foot."

"We're here to help you," said Bernard.

Tre Pound listened to them do their best to convince him to provide any information he had on Shelton's case. They weren't even here to talk about the cop murders; that charge was only mentioned as bait—they'd make it disappear if Tre Pound testified against his cousin. When Tre Pound said no, they offered to also do their best to get the statutory rape charge thrown out.

"We don't make these deals for everybody," said Bernard. "We normally require that cooperating witnesses still do some sort of time. Stop shaking your head, sit down, and talk to us, sir."

Tre Pound didn't even realize he was shaking his head. He was preoccupied with thoughts of the rape charge. That was the only thing that made him cringe. He could carry the cop murders on his back proudly, but the rape ... that would have been the only charge that made him cooperate—if he was a sucka.

"No disrespect to you two officers but, Can I go now?" he asked.

"Sure," said Bernard, standing up. "But think about the deal that's on the table. Prison or freedom. It's your choice."

***

The legs of Marlon's orange jumper rose when he sat down at Ms. Trisha Booker's desk, revealing faded orange socks. His jumper was a size too small. He didn't care. He folded his hands in his lap and waited for the questions.

"What's your name?" asked Trisha.

"Marlon Hayes," he said.

"Do you have any aliases?"

"No. I go by Marlon."

Ms. Trisha Booker couldn't see, but Marlon's knee was bouncing fast in front of her desk. He was anxious to meet up with Tre Pound. His heart was beating rapidly. He turned himself in so just so he could be face to face with Tre Pound.

When he saw on the news that Tre Pound was wanted for the cop killings, he started checking the Jackson County arrest records every other hour until he saw Tre Pound's name in the system. Marlon turned himself in immediately. He hated that they held him over 24 hours in the city jail. If they hadn't done that, he probably would have already been on Tre Pound's head by now.

"Well, it seems that no one has you listed as an enemy," said Trisha in a good-spirited chirp. "So that's a plus. Would you like me to list any enemies that you have?"

"No, ma'am," said Marlon. He leaned forward and put his elbows on his knees, trying to stop his leg from shaking. *Calm down,* he told himself. *You'll get him.*

"Are you in a gang?"

"No."

"What neighborhood are you from?"

"I'm from 51st Street."

She typed it in, then said, "It says here that your neighborhood is known for drug-trafficking, that you are enemies with 35th Street."

"That's not true. I have lots of friends from 35th Street."

She laughed. "So the drug-dealing is true?"

Marlon smiled. He hadn't smiled in a long time. A woman had to bring it out of him. "Can I ask a favor of you?"

"I'm not allowed to do favors, but what is it?"

"I have a real good friend of mines that's incarcerated here. He's actually from 35th Street. His name is Levour King. If you could put me in the same module as him, I'd greatly appreciate it."

"He's your friend?"

"He's like my brother."

Trisha tapped on her keyboard, hit enter, then looked interested by what she saw on her screen. "Levour King just got here. He has a boatload of enemies too." She sighed. "I think it would be a good idea for you and him to be wing-mates. We try to group people together that are friends with each other to keep the violence down. He's in 4A. I'll put you there, sure."

"Thank you, ma'am."

Both of Marlon's legs started shaking.

Chapter 24

Tre Pound was being let back inside 4A after his visit from the detectives. He waited for the door to open up. He noticed the wing was in disarray before he walked all the way in. There were chess pieces scattered all on the floor, colorful Monopoly money strewn about. None of the inmates were trying to clean it up either. They were standing around, up against the wall or leaning on rails. A couple of them were standing in their cell doorways, looking nervous.

Everyone seemed to be waiting for something to happen.

Tre Pound found Lil' Pat by the phones, not talking on it but sort of guarding it. Or maybe the phones were guarding him. He looked apprehensive like the rest, as if he was about to dial 911.

"What happened while I was gone?" Tre Pound asked him.

Lil' Pat pointed to a cell on the top tier. A whole twin mattress suddenly came flying out. It landed on top of one of the metal tables.

"Whose cell is that?" Tre Pound asked.

"Kenneth's," said Lil' Pat. "He got a life sentence. It finally hit him that he's never getting out of jail. He snapped out not long after you left for your visit."

"Yall are just letting him tear up the module?"

"Everybody is letting him vent."

"It looks to me like everybody is scared. I'm not about to let this nigga fuck up where I gotta live. Fuck this shit. Until I get a bond, I plan to live in peace."

Tre Pound mounted the metal steps to the top tier. He stopped just outside Kenneth's cell, leaned against the doorway with his arms crossed and watched Kenneth plop down on the metal bed frame that jutted out the wall. Kenneth moaned. He slapped his hands on his head frustratedly, then clenched them into fists and started beating on his own skull.

Tre Pound reached in the cell and knocked on the wall.

Kenneth's head jerked up. "What the fuck do you want?"

"I just wanted to know when are you gonna get around to cleaning all that shit you fucked up?"

"I'm not cleaning a damn thing! Those punk-ass guards can come in and clean it."

"You already know they're gonna make us inmates do it. Just clean it up and get it over with. I know you got a life sentence and all that, but you still gotta respect yo fellow inmates. If not everybody else, you damn sure better respect me."

Kenneth stared at Tre Pound angrily for a moment, then his eyes suddenly lit up with an idea. He stood to his feet and brushed past Tre Pound and ran down the steps and over to the gaping module window. He knocked on it, then waved his arms to get the attention of somebody in the wing across the hall.

DISOBEYISH

Tre Pound didn't know what this fool was doing. He walked down the steps after him, mentally preparing for a fight. *Hurt him but don't kill him,* Tre Pound thought to himself, flexing his fingers as he walked casually over to where Kenneth was hand-signaling someone. *You have to hurt him, though. All these people watched him disrespect you by running past you like he heard nothing you just said. You're a King. Everyone in here needs to know how Kings get down.*

Hurt him. Hurt him bad.

As Tre Pound got closer he saw who Kenneth was signaling. It was bank robber Tommy. The silent conversation must have been over now because Tommy held up his thumb, as if giving Kenneth some kind of approval. Kenneth turned, and was a tad bit startled by how close Tre Pound was standing.

The surprise went away quickly. Kenneth stared at Tre Pound with a deadly glare in his eyes.

"Are you done talking to your buddy?" Tre Pound said. "Because I need you to get started on that sweeping."

Kenneth pulled out a knife and Tre Pound took a step back. The blade was crude; it shined like aluminum foil molded into a pointy tip. There was no hilt, just torn white fabric wrapped around an end which acted as a handle.

Lil' Pat intervened, grabbing Kenneth's arm. "No, Kenneth. Tre Pound is my ex-girlfriend's cousin. He's not—"

Kenneth swiped his arm back and tore a slice through the sleeve of Lil' Pat's jumper. Lil' Pat let out a noise that was between a cry and a croak, as he fell to the floor out of fright. He clutched his arm as if it had been ripped open. But when he looked through the hole in his sleeve, there

163

was just a tiny sliver of blood. The cut had barely broke the skin. Any deeper, though, and he'd be in trouble.

Kenneth waved the knife back at Tre Pound. The tip boasted a tiny dot of red. "I got a lot of time to do now," he said to Tre Pound. "So that means I'ma need lots of money for commissary. Tommy just upped the ante another fifty grand. So that means I get a quarter million if I kill you right now."

"Tommy won't pay you," Tre Pound said, taking another step back.

"I think he will."

Kenneth swiped the blade at Tre Pound, missing his stomach by inches. The mere sound of the blade swiping through the air told Tre Pound it was sharp, not to mention the demonstration on Lil' Pat, who was curled up in the corner, breathing rapidly, clutching the tear in his sleeve as if he'd been shot.

Tre Pound was walking backwards, and Kenneth followed at the same pace. Inmates gave them room. One tripped over a chair as he scrambled to move out of the way. Others watched raptly from a safe distance. The module grew silent.

"Do you know who I am?" Tre Pound asked. He started walking up the stairs backwards.

"I don't care," Kenneth growled.

On the top tier, Tre Pound looked behind him and saw he had nowhere to go. Unless he jumped over the rail. But by doing that he could risk breaking an ankle. Then Kenneth could just waltz down the steps and stab him to death. Another option Tre Pound had was to run inside a cell and slam the door locked. But he quickly dismissed that idea as soon it entered his mind.

I can't run. Kings don't retreat.

"Fight me head up," Tre Pound said. "Put the knife down."

"Nah, I like easy money," Kenneth said, approaching faster.

Then someone banged on the module window and both Tre Pound and Kenneth looked. There was a guard yelling something through the glass. From his motions it was clear he was telling Kenneth to put the knife down. The relief Tre Pound felt was like a narcotic flowing through him.

Until Kenneth jabbed the knife in his stomach.

"Aargh!" Tre Pound groaned in agony. Instinctively, he grabbed Kenneth's hand so he couldn't yank the blade back out.

Kenneth shoved it in further, then twisted it with a *crunch*, and in that moment of tortuous pain, Tre Pound cried out and instantly head-butted him.

Kenneth stumbled backwards and paused. He touched his nose. It was bleeding.

"Good one," Kenneth smiled.

Kenneth came at him again, tried to grab the knife out of Tre Pound's stomach. Tre Pound let him run into him, but managed to get low enough to grab Kenneth's legs.

It happened in one smooth motion:

Tre Pound lifted up; Kenneth went airborne; Tre Pound twisted his body, his torso exploding with pain; Kenneth went over the rail; Tre Pound let go; Kenneth was freefalling to his death.

He landed on his back, smacking the metal table with a booming *throng*.

Then, astonishingly, Kenneth rolled over onto his side. But he was so weak and disoriented that he continued to roll—he rolled right off the table onto the concrete floor, hit his head hard. He was out cold.

"Oh shit!" an inmate squelched.

Tre Pound's knees gave out all of a sudden, and he fell against the wall, sinking to the floor. He wanted to pull the knife out *so bad* but knew it would only make his situation worse. The blood was thickening his jumper, pumping through it. As the guards stormed into the module, he had a foreboding feeling that he wasn't going to make it.

I'm dying!

Gasping for breath, Tre Pound was suddenly lifted to his feet by two guards. He cradled his hand around the rag-handle of the knife, protecting it, and then hobbled along the concrete tier with his escorts. Going down the steps was a feat. He lost his footing twice, but the guards held him up.

"You did that shit, Tre Pound."

"That was gangsta shit!"

"You fucked that nigga up, homie."

Tre Pound turned to see his fellow inmates cheering him on. A couple of them were pumping their fists in the air. There were smiles all across the module.

"Kenneth deserved that shit," someone said.

"I wish you would've killed him."

"Hold yo head up, gangsta!"

Three or four inmates started clapping.

Tre Pound was in pain, but somehow—maybe it was the adrenaline, or the sudden surge of triumph powering through him—he started to feel as if the pain was less intense. His breathing eased, and he courageously went against the alarm of his muscle sensors and looked over his shoulder at all the inmates in his line of sight.

"King shit," he said to them with the best smile he could muster.

Chapter 25

As soon as Marlon Hayes entered the wing, he tossed his box to the floor and stalked inside the first cell he saw looking for Tre Pound.

There was an old man laying on a bunk reading a hand-written letter. The man lifted his leg defensively upon seeing Marlon.

"Hey ... I didn't do shit. What's-what did I—what's the problem, youngblood?" the old man stammered.

Marlon skipped to the next cell. It was empty. The cell after that was empty too.

"Get the fuck out my cell!" someone behind him yelled.

Marlon looked. Some brotha standing near the TV with a T-shirt tied around his head had said it. The brotha wasn't Tre Pound so Marlon went on to the next cell.

Inside was a young guy who was sitting at his desk writing. His back was turned. He was the same complexion as Tre Pound.

Marlon grabbed his shoulder and spun him around.

"What the fuck is wrong with you, nigga?!" The guy shot to his feet. He was holding his pencil like a shank. "What the fuck are you in my cell for?"

It wasn't Tre Pound, Marlon observed sullenly. This guy looked similar to him in height, skin tone, and build, but it wasn't him.

Marlon said, "The lady down there in intake told me Tre Pound was in this wing. Where is he?"

"I don't fucking know. But I do know you better take yo light-skinned, bushy-face bum ass out my cell before I fuck you up."

Marlon walked out, went and stood on one of the metal tables in the center of the wing. He looked down at his feet curiously. There were red spots on the table he was standing on. *Blood?* he wondered. *Where'd it come from?* Ignoring the thought, he looked up and took in all the inmates standing about and staring at him like he'd lost his mind.

"Where THE FUCK is TRE POUND?!" Marlon roared.

"They took him out," said Lil' Pat.

Marlon looked at him.

"They took him to medical. He got into a fight."

"How long ago?" Marlon asked.

"About two hours ago. Somebody stabbed him. Do you remember me? I'm Lil' Pat."

"I remember you. You used to talk to Tre Pound's little cousin Camille. Yo big brother is Hoodey." Marlon jumped down off the table. He gave Lil' Pat dap. "Who stabbed Tre Pound?"

"This guy named Kenneth Shuman. He was supposed to be looking out for me. Him and Tre Pound got into it like five minutes after Tre Pound stepped in the wing. Then, today, Kenneth got sentenced to life in prison and tried to collect on the money from the contract on Tre Pound's head. It didn't go so well."

Marlon cursed under his breath. "How do I get to medical?"

Lil' Pat shrugged. "I don't know. I guess you have to have some kind of medical problem."

One way or another, Marlon had to get to medical.

"Hit me," Marlon said.

Lil' Pat looked confused. "Do what?"

"Punch me in my fucking face."

"I can't do that."

"You can too. I got money. I'll put it on yo books. They're not gonna have me in here long. I'm only in on a probation violation for skipping out on my house arrest. As soon as I get out I'll put $200 on yo books. Or a thousand. No, *two thousand*. Whatever you want."

"Marlon, are you okay? Why are you trying to find Tre Pound so bad? And when did you grow a beard? You was always a clean-cut type of guy, with glasses. Pretty boy, like me."

"Punch me!"

"No. I already got money on my books."

Marlon cold-cocked him in the mouth, made his head snap back. Lil' Pat went down, right on his butt. Holding his mouth, he looked up at Marlon in near tears.

"Marlon, I'm not gonna hit you back. You're my friend. We're supposed to stick together in here—"

Marlon kicked him in the leg. "Get up and fight me!"

Someone from behind shoved Marlon. It was the guy with the shirt tied around his head. He was taller than Marlon and outweighed him also.

"Stop picking on that little nigga," said T-shirt head. "I dare you to try to pick on me."

Another inmate came and stood beside him. "We don't

play that bully shit in this module," he said. "Take that shit down the hall."

"Push the button!" an inmate yelled at Marlon from the top tier. Marlon looked up. This inmate—not tall or hefty, but muscular in his own right—was gripping the rail as if he was agile enough to jump over it and land safely enough to come attack Marlon. "Push that panic button on the wall. The guards will come escort you out of here. Because like the man just told you, we don't play that bully shit."

Marlon grinned at these men in the same orange as him, grinned at each and every one of them. This was what he needed!

Swiftly, Marlon charged at T-shirt head and tackled him to the ground. He stole a punch, snatched off his T-shirt to reveal a head of remarkable wavy hair and then—even though Marlon didn't really want to—he tried to strangle him with his own T-shirt.

An inmate pulled him off, as Marlon hoped one would.

"Not on my watch," the inmate said, tying Marlon's hands above his head in a nelson hold.

Marlon gave weak attempts to get free—he squirmed a little, but put no real might into it. Actually, Marlon wasn't sure if he could pull loose even if tried to. The inmate who had him in the hold was cock strong.

T-shirt head—who could no longer be called T-shirt head because Marlon had yanked it off—stood up and punched Marlon in the gut. Marlon gagged. *God, he hits hard!* The second punch was so painful that Marlon wasn't sure if a lung collapsed.

"Okay," Marlon panted, spitting on the floor. He was hanging limply, but still being held up from behind. "That's enough. Call the nurse."

"Oh, I'm just getting started," said the inmate formerly known as T-shirt head.

"No, I'm done. Please, I'm trying get to Tre—"

He was cut off by yet another punch to the gut. A half minute later, Marlon was coughing up blood.

Chapter 26

Tre Pound swashed his tongue around inside his mouth. He was trying to think of what flavor it was, because there was no label on the yogurt the nurse had given him.

He thought on it for a minute longer, letting the bland taste settle.

Coconut, he decided.

"Mr. King, how are you feeling?" the nurse asked as she entered his room. She was dressed in navy blue scrubs. White lady with a dark brown ponytail, young eyes, but she still looked older than Tre Pound. She had bad skin—dull white and blotchy, with remnants of severe acne that had just recently gotten better. Her smile, though, was inviting and young and fresh, like her eyes.

She was jail cute, in Tre Pound's opinion. But not street cute. Her name was Ashley Hitzig.

"My stomach still feels fucked up," Tre Pound said. "Just when I start thinking the pain is going away, it pounces back with a vengeance."

"The knife didn't go that deep, or puncture any popular organs. The blade was sharp but way too thick."

"Tell that to my stomach."

"We're releasing you back to population in a few hours."

"What? No. I just got here."

The prison hospital, sometimes referred to as Medical, had been good to Tre Pound. Since being stitched up, he'd been afforded all the comforts he could ask for in jail. A mattress that reclined, free yogurt, and alternating nurses waiting on him hand and foot.

"We need bed space," Ashley said apologetically. "There's fights every day in here, inmates in worse condition than you that need our immediate attention. Our beds are full so we can't keep you. I'm sorry, Mr. King."

"I have enemies, though. Check my file. I can't go back out in population like this. I can't defend myself like this."

"That's why we're putting you in a medical wing. All the inmates in that wing are recovering from some sort of trauma."

"This is inhumane."

"It is. I'm not saying it's not."

"I'ma write the governor," Tre Pound joked.

Ashley Hitzig smiled. "Ask him about pay raises for me, will you?"

"Can I use the phone to call my lawyer?"

"Sure. Can you walk to it?"

"I don't wanna risk it."

Tre Pound sat up, as Ashley wheeled his bed over a few feet so he wouldn't have to walk. She positioning him right under the wall phone, and Tre Pound took it off the hook and called his lawyer, Miron Schnoll.

"Hello, Mr. King."

"Did Buttercup drop you off the money?"

"She did. Nice friendly gal you got there."

"Any good news?" Tre Pound asked.

"Yes, yes. You have a court date tomorrow morning.

I have a strong feeling they're gonna give you a bond on the rape charge."

Tre Pound cringed every time he heard it. *Rape charge.* It was embarrassing, degrading, emasculating. *Rape charge.* He was lumped in the same category as men who violently took pussy. He needed this off his record fast.

"What do you mean by *strong feeling?"* Tre Pound asked. "You should know if they're gonna let me go or not."

"There's no way of knowing what the judge will concede to, Mr. King."

Tre Pound clenched his jaw. *If Carlo Masaccio was my lawyer I'd be out of here by now,* he thought. *Is this part of Shelton's plan? Is Miron Schnoll a plant whose job it is to keep me locked up long enough for one of these scumbucket inmates to kill me?*

"Are you still there, Mr. King?"

"Yeah, I'm here. Check this out. If you don't get me out of here by tomorrow night, you're fired."

"Mr. King," Miron Schnoll began. "I'm doing my best—"

Tre Pound hung up on him. Laying back on the comfy incline, he tried to think positive about making it out of the county jail alive. He hoped it wasn't wishful thinking. So far in his life he'd survived a near-death gun battle at Camille's talent show, being chased through the 50s as Marlon unloaded from an assault rifle, a knife puncture through the hand and shoulder—compliments of Buttercup—and now a stabbing to the stomach from a lifer. There had been countless other times he'd been shot at or held at gunpoint, but only a few times where he felt "this is it." Too many more days in this county and it could really *be it.*

Tre Pound took a deep breath—or tried to anyway. He felt that sharp pain again in his midsection halfway through the inhalation. He couldn't even breathe right! And they wanted to put him in a medical wing? What if he ran into an enemy down there?

"Man, this is fucked up," he said.

Then, as a way to allay his low spirits, his thoughts shifted to the cheers from the inmates in 4A. His skin started tingling just thinking about it. He could hear their praise in his head now, as if they were standing in this room with him at this very moment. *Hold yo head up, gangsta. You did that shit, Tre Pound.*

Smiling at the memory, he leaned back up in bed and grabbed his yogurt cup and plastic spoon and scraped up what was left.

This is some damn good coconut.

Chapter 27

There was only one medical wing in the entire Jackson County Detention Center. It was located on the third floor. That's where they stuck Marlon Hayes. He was in his cell, laying down, staring up at the ceiling and trying not to move too much.

But he reared up in his bed when a violent cough seized him. When the fit was over, he looked at the napkin he had pressed to his mouth.

Spots of blood all over it. But not as much as before, and for that he was thankful. His last few napkins, which he'd flushed down the toilet, had been soiled with blood.

"They should've held you overnight in medical."

Marlon looked over and saw a crippled inmate in a wheelchair blocking his doorway. It was an older man he had never seen before.

"But you know why they didn't admit you, right?" the man said.

"Why?" Marlon asked.

"Because medical is probably full. No more bed space. Denying you, though, is against policy. They're stipulated by law to provide every inmate with immediate medical attention as needed."

"I'm not worried about it," Marlon said. He coughed into his napkin again. "I don't plan on being here long."

The man wheeled himself into the cell. "My name's Tony," he said, holding out his hand.

Marlon shook it. "Marlon Hayes."

"What happened to you, Marlon? Police beat you up? I know a little bit about the law and can point you in the right direction if you're thinking about a lawsuit. I help everybody who comes in this wing ... for a small fee, of course. Just a couple snacks off commissary is all I ask. I'm not gon' rob you."

"I'm good. Police didn't beat me up. I got jumped by some niggas in 4A."

Tony's eyes narrowed curiously. "By who?"

"I don't know. I don't even care."

"Was it Tre Pound?"

Marlon tensed, and unknowingly balled his fists and crushed his napkin. His eyes were scrutinizing Tony. "Why'd you ask that?"

"My brother Tommy is in the wing across the hall. He told me there's a guy named Tre Pound in 4A, and I wanted to know if you—"

"I know Tre Pound," Marlon said, cutting him off. "He's sort of the reason I'm in here."

"You're kidding me? He snitched on you?"

"He killed my sister."

Tony shook his head sadly. "I'm sorry to hear that. Tre Pound is the reason I'm in this wheelchair. Somebody he was with rammed their car into my legs, smashed 'em up into bits. Then he shot me in the head. I'm lucky to still be alive."

Tony's mangled legs stopped at the knees, where his

orange jumper was knotted up and stapled. Marlon tried not to stare.

Tony continued. "What kicked the incident off was Tre Pound's ignorance. He accused me of lying when I told him his cousin Gutta was a confidential informant. But I got the paperwork to prove that Gutta is a rat. Tre Pound wasn't trying to hear it though ... and shit got ugly." Tony rested his elbows on the arms of his wheelchair and intertwined his fingers in his lap. It was a formal posture, the way a president would sit before making a big announcement. "Me and my brother Tommy have been robbing banks since 1997. Feds couldn't catch us in the act. We were untouchable. We were legendary in Kansas City. You've probably heard of us."

Marlon had heard of them. The names Tommy and Tony were synonymous with bank robbery. Marlon was surprised that this was the same Tony sitting in front of him whom he'd heard, as a kid, had shot three off-duty cops during a getaway. It was disheartening to see him in a wheelchair now.

But Marlon wasn't about to stroke his ego. He kept listening as if he didn't have a clue who he was.

"I'm not trying to brag, but me and my brother are the best at what we do," Tony said. "We don't make mistakes. It took a C.I. named Maurice 'Gutta' King to bring us down. I heard Gutta got murdered already—not for snitching on me, but for snitching on his own cousin Shelton. Gutta got his karma. Tre Pound needs to get his."

"He will," Marlon said.

"So Tre Pound wasn't in 4A at the same time you were?"

"No. A nigga that was in there told me Tre Pound had just been pulled out. Somebody stabbed him."

Tony looked shocked. "Killed him?"

"Nah, I don't think so."

"Oh wow. That means he's in medical, and they'll be putting him in this wing any day now." Tony leaned forward. "Marlon, listen to me. There was a hundred thousand dollars in the air for the death of Tre Pound. Last time I talked to my brother, he told me he upped it another hundred grand. That money is yours if you beat him down enough for me to kill him myself. I'm not going home, Marlon. These pigs are gonna give me and my brother life. You don't have to kill Tre Pound; let me do it. Just get him on the ground where he can't move none, and I'll finish him. I'll take the blame for it all and you can go home."

"Tony, I'm not worried about going home," Marlon said. "I'm doing this for my sister."

"Please let me get in on the action. Please."

"I can't promise you that."

A noise caught both of their attention. It was the heavy mechanical sound of the module door opening. Someone was being let inside the wing. Tony rolled to the front of Marlon's cell and looked out.

He gasped. "Speak of the devil ..."

Marlon shot to his feet, then instantly regretted it. His ribs screamed for him to sit back down. Stubbornly, he walked with a slight limp over to see what Tony was seeing.

It was Tre Pound!

Tony said, "Stay here, Marlon. I'm gonna distract him to make sure you get the first punch. It looks like you're gonna need it."

***

Tre Pound entered the medical wing accompanied by a correctional officer who was carrying his property box for him. The C.O. dropped the box flat on the floor.

"You're not gonna carry it to my cell for me?" Tre Pound asked, scowling at him.

"Hell no."

"The nurse told me not to carry nothing' that weighs more than twenty pounds."

"Just have one of your fellow inmates carry it the rest of the way. That is, if you can find one that's not fucked up too." The C.O. laughed, then stepped back behind the module door as it began to close.

When the lock clicked shut, Tre Pound knew he was trapped here—trapped in another module with a bunch of inmates who looked to be in worse shape than him. Several inmates were on crutches. Two inmates playing dominos against each other looked like they'd been in the same melee—one was wearing an eye patch, and the other inmate's right eye was indented with purple bruising so severe that the whites of his eye had gone black.

Out of nowhere, someone from a cell on the top tier let out a moan that was both painful and ghostly.

Tre Pound shook his head. *I hope Miron gets me out of here tomorrow,* he mused.

He started to take a step toward the phones when he felt a sudden pang in his calf. A man in a wheelchair had bumped into him.

"Watch where the fuck you going, old head!" Tre Pound snapped.

"Fuck you. You rammed me, I ram you."

Tre Pound identified him at once.

Tony the Bank robber. *Ol' Tony.*

Tre Pound smiled. "I thought you was dead."

"You can't kill me that easily. You and yo people are gonna have to come a lot harder than that to take me out."

"Get the fuck out of here. Nigga, *you* probably thought you was dead too."

Tony stared up at him. "You should've listened to me."

"What?"

"About yo cousin Gutta. If you would've listened to me when I told you he was a C.I., then Shelton would still be on the streets."

Tre Pound snatched Tony up by his orange collar and would have picked him all the way up out of his seat if Tony hadn't grabbed the wheelchair arms.

"I don't wanna hear shit about either one of my cousins come out yo mouth!" Tre Pound barked in his face. "Whatever Gutta did is family business. We handled it. So if you don't wanna get handled, then you'll let that shit go. I could be dragging you across the floor for shooting at me, but I'm not. You need to stop worrying about me and mines and focus more on counting yo blessings."

Tre Pound let him drop back in the seat.

"Yo time is coming," Tony said fearlessly. "You're gonna pay for all the shit you've done to people."

"You think so? Why's that, because you're paying for yo shit now? You old niggas kill me. Ain't nobody made me pay for shit yet, have—?"

Something dark flashed past Tre Pound's eyes and immediately went around his neck. He was being strangled from behind. Choking, he grabbed the material that was constricting his throat—a trashbag?—and tried to pull it away and get some air. He got a scant of a breath, but then the bag was yanked tighter and he gagged.

Then Marlon's voice hissed in his ear: "I wanna hear you cry, muthafucka. Go ahead and let them tears fall." Marlon pulled harder. "This is love right here. It feels so good to hear you squeaking for air. *Squeak, squeak.* You're like my little mouse."

As Tre Pound struggled, he thought he felt something poking him in the buttocks. Was it an erection? *It is an erection!* Marlon was getting turned on by killing him!

Tre Pound panicked. He pushed backwards mightily, forced Marlon to go backwards as well. In the same motion Tre Pound hooked his leg behind Marlon's, killing both their balance, and they went down hard.

Suddenly, Tre Pound could breathe again!

As soon as he got to his feet he stumbled against the wall, rubbing his own throat as if to loosen it up. It was then that he saw that Marlon was still on the ground, holding his side and writhing in agony. Marlon actually started coughing up blood.

Did I just do that? Tre Pound wondered with a growing smile. He walked over and kicked Marlon in his ribs. A spatter of blood shot out of his mouth.

"You had to sneak up behind me, huh?" Tre Pound taunted, and when he kicked him again he felt something inside Marlon's chest give way. "Couldn't fight me head up, huh? And you called *me* a bitch?"

"I'ma ... kill you," Marlon moaned.

"I just don't see that happening. But you did give it a helluva shot, which is more than I can say about a lot of these niggas that claim they funkin' wit' me."

"Muthafuckin' pussy ..."

Tre Pound hiked up his orange pants legs and squatted down beside Marlon. It hurt his stomach to be bent down like this but he tried not to show it. He put on a smile and patted Marlon's ribs like he was a lap dog. "That's all you got left in you, huh? Name-calling? I'ma do you a favor when I get outta here, because I should be able to make bond tomorrow. I'ma go to yo parents' gravesite and tell them who the real pussy is, so you won't have to do it."

Marlon reached out and grabbed a fistful of Tre Pound's pants leg, as if to pull him down to his level. Tre Pound didn't budge.

"And I do know where yo parents are buried," Tre Pound assured him. "Dominique showed me. There's a bench that sits right in front of their tombstones, right? Yeah, me and Dominique christened it. I took her virginity on that bench. Piped her down real good. On my 'hood, I fucked the shit outta Dominique like the bitches me and you used to run through."

Tre Pound heard a noise behind him and turned reflexively, and in a miraculous show of strength he saw Tony propelling himself out of his wheelchair. The legless man landed on Tre Pound's back and wrapped his arms around his neck in a choke hold. Tre Pound couldn't support the weight. They went down together.

"You're not gonna get away!" Tony shrieked. "Not today!"

Tony had his neck tied up good. Tre Pound tugged on his arms but the power in his biceps was uncanny—all that rolling around in the wheelchair gave ol' Tony superior upper-body strength. Tre Pound was losing air fast.

"Go to sleep!" Tony hissed. "So I can make sure you never wake up again. Go to sleep, lil' nigga!"

Tre Pound blinked against his will, several times. His lids were fluttering. He couldn't keep them open! His eyes danced around the module for help, but all he was seeing was blurs of orange everywhere, crippled inmates just standing about watching him suffer. Tre Pound blinked again, and his eyes stayed shut longer than he'd wanted to. When he forced them open again, he saw Marlon standing over him with a mop handle.

The last thing Tre Pound saw before he passed out was Marlon raising the stick above his head.

Swack!

Chapter 28

Camille woke up early this morning with a gameplan. And every gameplan needed a name. Hers was called *Operation Love Tre Pound.*

On her bed, in the little room Buttercup had provided, she had her notes spread out in front of her. Since six this morning she'd been compiling facts about love, the uncertainty of it, historical accounts of people going against tradition in love's name, the fact that love was in and of itself a thought process that stemmed from the heart, and if not the heart then the brain, and that right there should tell any logical person—like Tre Pound— that love started from within and reached outward, not the other way around. She would explain to him that outsiders should have no influence on his decision whether or not to love her.

Any and everything that supported her agenda she wrote it down.

Tre Pound's main argument was he couldn't love her simply because "it was wrong," that she was his cousin. She had a rebuttal for that. Second paragraph down on her historical sheet she had copied a passage about the House of Habsburg, a dynasty that occupied the Holy Roman

Empire from the fifteenth century onward. Its rulers were full of closely related unions.

"They did it for love and political reasons," Camille practiced out loud. "And also for purity. Our baby will be a pure King if we keep it. Back then, way before modern day, our love wouldn't even be taboo. It was only frowned upon by non-royals. But we're Kings, Tre Pound. We're royal all day."

She started leafing through the Bible for more notes to support her argument.

Then her bedroom door opened. Buttercup walked in uninvited. She was wearing what she'd fallen asleep in—white panties and a white bra full of impossibly large breasts. Camille couldn't help but stare at Buttercup's flawless body. It was unfair. Nothing was out of place, her waist curved perfectly down into athletic thighs, and she even got lucky enough to have "pussy gap."

Clearly, Buttercup walked in here half-naked to send Camille a message: *I'm a woman, you're not. I'm what Tre Pound desires.*

"What are you doing up so early?" Buttercup asked.

Camille placed the Good Book over her notes, hiding them. "I'm minding my own business," she said. "Something most people don't know how to do."

Frowning, Buttercup put her hands on her amazing hips. "Why are you trying to funk with me? I'm giving you a place to stay."

"For your information, I didn't choose to come here."

"Whether you chose to or not, you're still here."

"You want me to leave?"

Buttercup sighed. "No, I don't, Camille."

"Yes, you do. The only reason you're putting up with

me is because you know that's what Tre Pound wants. You don't have to be fake with me."

"It's too early for this. I gotta get ready for work."

Buttercup turned on her heels and started heading back out. Camille looked at her butt, the way it bounced, at how its magnitude still seemed symmetrical with her frame. Camille wasn't sure if Tre Pound liked the size of it or if it was just the way she walked.

I need to work on being more sexy, Camille thought.

She was only alone for a few minutes when her phone rang. It was a pre-paid call from Krystal.

"Hello?" Camille answered. "Krystal?"

"I'm here."

"How's it going? You sound like you've been crying."

"I have," Krystal said, sniffling. "I haven't gotten a letter yet from Moses. I think he's done with me."

"No, Krystal. He wrote you. I just haven't been able to send 'em off yet.

"He wrote me?"

"Yes. But I still don't have stamps because I've been moving around. I'm not at Bernice's anymore."

"You're not? Damn, I just sent another letter there."

"Well, hopefully they send it back to you and then you can send it to my new address."

"Where are you living now?"

"I'm at a bitch named Buttercup's house. One of Tre Pound's groupies. Me and Bernice got into it and she kicked me out. It's been a lot of craziness going on that I can't talk about over the phone. One thing I can tell you, though, is that Tre Pound got locked up."

"Oh my God, they're rounding everybody up. I'm never gonna get out of here."

"You will. You just have to be patient. Remember, you didn't do anything. You're just bait. They'll let you go after Shelton's trial."

"Has Marlon called you?"

"I've had one missed call from him," Camille lied.

"I guess that's good. That means he's thinking about me."

Camille grew more worried about Krystal every time she talked to her. Jail wasn't a place for good people like her. Krystal was a giver; she'd give her last, even to people she didn't know. Camille and Dominique rescued Krystal in high school, but there was nothing that could be done now. The girls in the juvenile center were probably running all over her.

Unannounced once again, Buttercup barged into the room. She was fully dressed now. "Can I talk to you before I leave for work?" she asked.

"I'm on the phone."

"Can't you call them back?"

"It's a jail call."

"Tre Pound?"

"No, my friend Krystal."

Buttercup looked at her watch, then leaned against the wall with her arms crossed. "Okay, I'll wait."

Camille rolled her eyes, then told Krystal to call back in a half hour. Then she eyed Buttercup, looking intentionally at her work clothes. Buttercup looked a lot better naked.

"I'm off the phone," Camille said. "What do you want?"

"I wasn't gonna bring this up but I feel I have to," Buttercup started. "I know what's going on between you and Tre Pound. It's plain as day."

"What are talking about?"

188

"Yall two are fuckin' each other."

Camille's eyes got wide and her heart started beating faster. *Did Tre Pound tell her?* Camille didn't know what to say.

"We ... No, we're not."

Buttercup laughed once. "You suck at lying. It's written all over your face, honey. I'm not standing here asking you if it's true. I know it's true. He calls me your name during sex."

He does?! Camille thought excitedly. She swallowed to keep herself from smiling.

"I just wanna give you some advice, from a female who knows what you're feeling. Can I do that?"

"I'm just sitting here listening to yo dumb ass talk."

"I'm far from dumb. I've been to college. I write poetry in my free time and try to learn new things every day. I don't know it all, but I do know you're kidding yourself. What you and Tre Pound got going on won't last. It's just a phase he's going through. And when it's over, you're gonna be left with a crushed heart in your hand."

"Sounds like he did you like that."

"He has. And he continues to break my heart. But the difference between me and you is I'm not a little girl. He knows I'm capable of handling him, that's why he keeps coming back to me. But I'm realizing now what's keeping him from committing to me. It's you."

"Bitch, you're crazy."

"I might be. But this crazy bitch won't stop loving Tre Pound. I'ma be here. Always. He's only fuckin' you because it's convenient."

Camille stood up. "He loves me, bitch!"

"I'm not saying he doesn't. He's your cousin, he was raised with you, he's supposed to love you. But that kind of love has a cap on it. That love will never come close to what he experiences with a female like me. For your own sake, you need to stop fuckin' him. You're confusing him. And you're confusing yourself."

"I never forced him to do anything."

"I doubt that."

"He's mine!"

"You sound childish. You'll never compare to me, little girl. I've competed with and crushed a lot of bitches behind Tre Pound. You're not even in the same league as his worst bitch. You're just pretty. You don't even know how to switch your hips yet. I've seen you walk. Nothing sexy about it. You still wear tennis shoes, for God's sake. The only reason you're getting dick from him is because you're related. He's giving you hand-outs."

Camille tried to punch her, but Buttercup caught her wrist and bent her arm unnaturally. Camille shrieked in pain.

"Let me go!"

"I'm not playing with you, little girl. Stop fuckin' my man!"

"Let me go! You're gonna break my arm!"

"This is my warning to you. Don't ever touch Tre Pound's nuts again. You already have his love as his cousin. Stop being greedy."

Buttercup finally released her and she shrank away, holding her sore wrist.

"I have to go to work," Buttercup said. "Think about our talk. I don't wanna funk with you. But I will."

Buttercup left the room, throwing emphasis on her strut. Camille launched to her feet and went after her. In a rage, Camille grabbed the vase and yanked it off the coffee table, popping the plug out the socket. Buttercup was turning to investigate the sound when Camille smashed the vase in her face.

Buttercup went down like a rag doll. Camille straddled her and yelled in her bloody face.

"You don't know me, bitch! You don't know what me and Tre Pound have been through!"

Buttercup was barely conscious. Camille picked up one of the ceramic shards and without hesitating she stabbed Buttercup in the face over and over. Sheets of blood poured out the lacerations. She two-handed the shard, hammering down hard enough to tear through nose bone and mandible. This was payback for stabbing Tre Pound, she told herself as she left the shard sticking in Buttercup's eye socket.

Nothing more than payback.

Camille sucked in a few deep breaths, as she took in all the blood around her, on her own hands and skin, splattered over the gouges in Buttercup's face. It was a mess. A lot more messy than how she murdered Dominique.

Still straddling the corpse, she looked up at the clock on the wall. In a couple hours Tre Pound was supposed to be in court.

Come home to me, baby, Camille pleaded silently. *Please come home to me.*

Chapter 29

"You must have missed me," Ashley Hitzig smiled.

Tre Pound could only open one of his eyes. He saw Ashley working his left arm into the sleeve of his jumper. She didn't get it through until he used his motor functions to help.

"Thank you," she said.

Tre Pound was back in the prison hospital, laying in bed looking down at the welts on his chest, until Ashley nudged his chin up so she could finish buttoning his jumper up to the neck.

"What happened to me?" Tre Pound asked.

"You got assaulted by a couple of inmates."

"How long have I been in here?"

"Overnight."

Tre Pound tried to sit up but his muscles started to explode with pain all throughout his upper body. He slammed back against the bed, hoping the pain stopped. It eased, but there was still a lingering, uncomfortable tingling sensation going on underneath his skin tissue.

"Don't sit up so fast," Ashley warned.

"I have to get to court," Tre Pound said with emergency. "I'm supposed to be getting out today."

"That's what I'm getting you dressed for. You're gonna make it to court, just chill. Take it easy. You'll make it hard on yourself if you get in a hurry."

The last thing Tre Pound remembered was hunkering down beside Marlon and making fun of him. He had bested him. Now, he was trying hard to picture what happened next, what left him like this, but for some reason his mind kept pushing forward images of Tony in his wheelchair laughing uncontrollably.

"They jumped me?" Tre Pound asked.

"We're not sure what happened or who was involved. They beat you pretty bad. Almost killed you. When the guards rushed in, there were several inmates fighting. One version of the story says you were being jumped, so inmates stepped in to stop it. There's like an unsaid code in the medical wing that forbids people from getting ganged up on. You guys in there are already wounded, so fights are supposed to be one-on-one."

"Some inmates helped me?"

"Yes, that's what a couple versions of the story say. But several other inmates said you jumped off the top tier of your own volition in an attempt to commit suicide. But your injuries just don't match up to that. Did you jump?"

"No."

"I didn't think so. A few of the inmates are claiming they didn't see a thing. So what I need you to do, Mr. Levour King, is ..." Ashley handed him a pen and clipboard. "... write down the names of the inmates who were involved. We'll put them on your enemy list and try to get some assault charges rolling. Then you're off to court."

Tre Pound looked at the clipboard. Attached to it was a mere blank sheet of notebook paper, not an authorized document. This was one of those snitch sheets.

He handed the clipboard back to her. "I think I did jump," he said.

***

Jackson County Courthouse

The judge picked up his reading glasses and peered through the lenses without putting them on. "Who's here representing Levour King?"

"I am, Your Honor," said Miron Schnoll, standing to his feet. He motioned for Tre Pound to come with him to the bench.

Grunting, Tre Pound stood his crutches up straight and used them to push himself to his feet. He could have really used a wheelchair. Ashley tried to get him one at the last minute, which was nice of her, but they were all checked out.

He got to the stand as best as he could, then slouched on the crutches for support. The judge looked him over with no pity.

"You're here before me today facing multiple charges. *Serious* charges. Apparently you've already bonded out on the murder of two police officers, which is an absurd thing, I might add. I'd hate to ask how you got the money to post it."

"Judge Harrell, my client received financial assistance from fam—"

The judge cut Miron off. "I don't wanna know, Mr. Schnoll. What I do wanna know is why you think your client also deserves to receive a bond on these statutory rape charges. I don't see myself letting this fly. Murder *and rape.* Why should this man be allowed back on the streets? Enlighten me."

Tre Pound was feeling heavier all of a sudden. Not because of fatigue, but because he was annoyed by that word the judge used. *Rape.* It irked the fuck out of him that he had to hold himself up and listen to this. He wasn't feeling kingly right now. And when he heard people whispering in the courtroom behind him, he just knew they were gossiping about him.

"Your Honor, my client has pleaded not guilty on those charges and should be treated as an innocent man until proven otherwise. That's what our principles state. But quite frankly I don't mind disregarding the presumption of innocence because my client *did not* commit these crimes. There's nothing to presume. He simply didn't do it, Your Honor. These are trumped up charges that are being leveraged against him to pressure him into testifying in another case."

"All the evidence I've seen looked strong," said Judge Harrell.

"We must be looking at different discoveries. Or maybe time only permitted you to skim over it. Because all the evidence I've seen—particularly pages 117 through 124—points to his innocence. Phone records in the cop case refute what the prosecutor is claiming. And on the alleged rape ..." Miron threw his hands up like he was bewildered by the entire courtroom. "The discovery on that is so small I was able to go through it in one sitting. The alleged underage victim in the case hasn't even been found, let alone interviewed and asked to identify my client. I believe they filed charges prematurely."

The judge assessed Tre Pound for a moment, then looked back at the lawyer.

Miron Schnoll continued. "We're here to request bond for two very significant reasons: one, my client has never been a flight risk; and two, he isn't safe in the Jackson County Detention Center. He has been stabbed and beaten by several different inmates on two different occasions, in separate parts of the jail. He also needs extended medical help that could become costly for the State if he remains incarcerated. Just take a look at him, Your Honor."

Tre Pound was studying Judge Harrell's facial expression—it told a story of a biased man won over by reason or duty. Tre Pound tried not to smile. Miron Schnoll was no Carlo Masaccio, but he was still something special.

Chapter 30

Miron Schnoll was behind the wheel of his Volvo, steering with one hand on the underside of the wheel. Tre Pound was in the passenger seat, staring out at the city as it passed by. His crutches were laying across the seat in the back.

Miron Schnoll waved a CD at Tre Pound teasingly. "So, do you wanna listen to it?"

"That's the tape?"

"Yes, sir, it is."

"How'd you get it?"

"It was sent to me, actually. Directly from Carlo Masaccio's office. I told you I have connections."

Connections? Tre Pound didn't see it that way. The CD was probably sent at Shelton's request. Shelton wanted Tre Pound to hear it, to send a message that the recording was real and that Tre Pound would have to pay for his actions.

"Put it in," Tre Pound said.

Miron slipped it in the stereo system.

The recording started with Tre Pound arguing with Camille about trying to leave town with Lil' Pat. Hearing an audio of himself gave him the chills. *What other recordings do they have?* he wondered. *Is the Infiniti the only property they bugged?* As the tape went on, and

Camille was heard crying after being told that her mother was murdered, Tre Pound began to feel the emotions from that day heat up inside him. He listened to himself defend against Camille's accusations that the murder was his fault, and he listened to himself reveal to her that Shelton gunned down Drought Man. He had incriminated Shelton on tape.

Fuck!

He shook his head regrettably, as he stared at the CD deck display. There was forty-one minutes of audio left.

"You didn't know you were being recorded," Miron stated. "Don't beat yourself up about it. Just focus on the words on this recording and how they can be used against you, not necessarily on what actually happened. Listen from a legal point of view. You need to think: What will the prosecutor grab from this and how can I disprove it?"

Tre Pound tried to listen objectively but it was difficult. When he heard Camille say, *Tre Pound you really love me and I really love you,* and then, *Tre it's big ... hard, I knew you wanted me bad too,* his heart started racing. He knew what was coming next. It flooded Miron's speaker system: the moans, the kissing sounds, Camille screaming in ecstasy accompanied by cars and trucks heard whizzing by in the background—it all brought him back to that highway roadside and the incredible way in which he came inside of his little cousin.

His dick was getting hard.

"Tre, I liked it," Camille said in a voice so clear it felt like she was here in the Volvo now.

The audio was superb.

Tre Pound paused the CD. "It's not enough to prove to a jury that I actually fucked her. You need video for that."

"Good. What else?"

198

"She didn't use my real name. I only used her first name. But there's still enough info on here to convince a jury that it was me and Camille in that car."

"We'll study the tape more later. There's a lot I have to look into on my end, like the legality of the tape. Did they have the proper approval to put that bug in your car in the first place? That's the big question. The answer to it could be the difference between trial and no trial."

"If they did record us illegally, then they wouldn't be able to use what I said about Shelton against him either, right?"

"It would be inadmissible."

Tre Pound pressed play and finished off the recording, then looped it back to the beginning. He kept wondering how Shelton must have felt when he was listening to it. Did he make it through the whole tape? Was it too sickening? Tre Pound could only imagine.

A moment later Miron parked the Volvo in front of Buttercup's house and said, "I'll contact you as soon as the next court date is scheduled."

"Thank you, Mr. Schnoll."

"Do you need help getting out?"

"I got it."

Tre Pound opened the door, lifted his legs up and out, and had to use the door to pull himself to his feet. Grabbing the crutches out the back, he positioned them under his arms and crutch-walked over to the front porch, and did just fine getting up the steps too. Behind him, Miron honked and drove off.

Tre Pound opened the screen door and let it close and hit him softly in the back, as he turned the knob and pushed open the front door. He crutch-walked inside.

Then he stopped.

"I almost got it cleaned up," Camille said, looking at Tre Pound for a second before turning her attention back to her scrubbing.

She was on her knees, wiping the blood off the floor with a bath towel. She wiped in big, hurried circles. Her jeans, at the knees, were dampened in blood the most, compared to the spatters on her shirt and hands, and the spots on her neck. The dead body—Buttercup's body—was draped over the couch out of the way, as if on punishment while Camille cleaned up her mess. There was evidence *everywhere*. And Camille kept making bigger swirls in the blood. She was making it worse.

"STOP!" Tre Pound roared.

Camille froze. She looked at him again, this time with concern. "What happened to you, Tre Pound? You're on crutches. Your face ..."

"Please tell me Buttercup's not dead, that you didn't kill her." Tre Pound's tone was pleading. "Please tell me that's not her blood."

"It's hers. It just kept pouring out of her. I'ma get it all up, though. Don't worry." She started making more swirls.

"I said STOP!"

Camille slouched back on her heels and dropped the towel in a puddle. She patted her thighs once. "You want me to just leave it?"

"Get the fuck up and change yo clothes. Now."

"You don't wanna know what happened?"

"DO IT NOW, Camille! We don't have time for this!"

Camille bounced to her feet and ran to her room. Tre Pound sat down on the end table, folding the crutches over his lap. His knees had gotten weak all of a sudden. He was overwhelmed.

I should've never left Camille here, he thought, as he fixed his mug on Buttercup's lifeless eyes—eyes that seemed to stare back at him. *I should've took Camille somewhere else. You're fucking stupid, Tre Pound. Another stupid-ass mistake ...*

Chapter 31

They got another hotel, a different one clear on the other side of town, in North Kansas City. It was an Econo Lodge on Taney Street. Tre Pound picked it because it was located in a part of town where he didn't have funk—or at least none he knew about. He was sitting on the dresser, staring at the bathroom door where shower water was running endlessly. He could feel the steam.

Camille was in there bathing.

He still hadn't asked her what happened because he didn't want to talk about it on the ride here. The Porsche was new, but who was to say the Feds hadn't already wired it? He had a good idea what happened anyway. Buttercup was jealous of Camille, so she tried Camille, and Camille outperformed.

I should've never brought Camille over there. Why the fuck did you do that, Tre Pound? Put two crazy girls that love you in the same house ...

The bathroom door opened. Camille came out in a blue pajama set, rubbing her curly wet hair with a towel, as if the tangles in her head were the most important thing in the world right now.

"Water pressure is low in there," she said.

She sat down on the bed in front of the dresser that Tre Pound was sitting on and rubbed some more, then set the towel aside. Her hair had gotten longer, Tre Pound noticed.

"Did you get it all off?" he asked.

"Yes." She showed him her hands, front and back. No trace of blood. "All gone," she said.

"What happened over there?"

"She tried to kill me."

Tre Pound studied her. "Out of the blue she tried to kill you?"

"Yes! Tre Pound, this is the same bitch that tried to kill you. What makes you think she wouldn't try to kill me?"

"She didn't have a reason to."

"In her head she did. She told me she knew that we fucked. She said you called out my name during sex, more than once. She was jealous of me."

"She told you that?"

"Yep. Right before she slammed that vase over my back. I grabbed one of the broken pieces and"—Camille pantomimed stabbing the air in one quick in-and-out motion—"*yocked* her ass in the face till she went down. She fucked with the wrong one."

"That's not true."

"It is too!"

"No, I'm talking about what she told you. I never said yo name while I was fucking her."

"Oh. Okay."

There was an awkward silence. Tre Pound got down off the dresser and walked to his bed without his crutches. He laid down, then looked over at Camille.

He said, "If you ever commit a crime and end up getting

fingerprinted, it's a ninety percent chance they'll match it to prints in Buttercup's house."

Camille shrugged. "Self-defense."

"That self-defense shit is iffy."

"Tell me what happened to you."

"I told you on the way over here. I got jumped."

"The guards didn't help you?"

He scoffed, then lifted his shirt so Camille could see the bandage on his stomach. She cringed, then gasped when he peeled the bandage back to reveal coagulated blood glued to the wound. It was dark dark red.

"Kenneth Shuman, a nigga I wasn't even funkin' wit', did this. I lobbed his ass off the top tier afterwards, though. Then I got jumped by Marlon and Tony in the medical wing."

"Marlon Hayes? Dominique's big brother? He was in there?"

"Yeah. I had him where I wanted him until Tony jumped in. You remember Tony; you ran him down with my Infiniti M and crushed his legs. He's in a wheelchair now."

"He lived? Gosh. Everybody we're funkin' wit' was in there."

Tre Pound noticed that she used the word *we're,* the contraction of *we are.* She was affirming his enemies as her own, and she seemed proud to.

He looked at her with respect. "In jail, you never know who you'll run into, Camille. Funk stops and starts in there."

***

Camille shuffled the deck, then dealt the cards out evenly between them.

"What are we playing this time?" Tre Pound asked, straightening up his set of cards.

"I Declare War," she said.

"You're lucky we don't have a chess board."

"No, *you're* lucky. You taught me how to play but I've gotten better."

They had been fooling around with the cards for a few hours now. Tre Pound was just wasting time, waiting on the breaking news story of Buttercup's homicide to pop up on the TV. It hadn't come yet, which meant her body hadn't been found or they were saving it for the ten o'clock news.

"Tre Pound, what are we doing?" Camille asked.

"Playing cards."

"I'm talking about this hotel. Why are we here?"

"Where else are we gonna go?"

"Out of town. Let's leave Kansas City."

"And go where?"

"Anywhere!"

"We got too many loose ends hanging. For one, we gotta wait on the news to find out what evidence they come up with at Buttercup's."

"Let's leave after that."

Tre Pound played a jack of diamonds that trumped Camille's nine of hearts. He added the cards to his deck. "I'm not letting nobody run me out of my city. That's how it would look. I got these cases I'm fighting, I got more money to collect—"

"You're scared," Camille interrupted. "You're scared of change. There's nothing left for us in Kansas City. Fuck those cases. The city is out to get you, Tre Pound. Not just the niggas in the streets, but those people in those offices too. They wanna see you behind bars. They're gonna keep charging you with shit you didn't do until something sticks. Let's just go!"

"On the run?"

"Yes! People do it all the time. We can start over. Shelton tried to kill you, Tre Pound. It's time to go. Our family has fallen apart."

"So what are we supposed to do, start a new King generation? Start with that baby your carrying?"

"We can. I'm down for it."

Tre Pound let out an amused snort. He played a card, a five of hearts. "We need to stop entertaining those thoughts. We're not leaving Kansas City, you're getting an abortion, and we're gonna fight it out with anybody that wants to funk with the Kings. We'll get out of this hotel when the time is right. Now play your card." He waited, then looked at her. "Play your card."

Camille stood up, crossing her arms over her chest. "I'm not getting an abortion. So if you wanna kill me, do it now." She shifted her weight to the other foot, daring him.

Tre Pound would have stood up fast but his body wasn't in good enough condition. So he took his time, pressing his hand tight against his injured stomach. He got in her face.

"You want me to put my hands on you?"

"I'm not scared of you, Tre Pound. You might be able to beat me down, but I'ma give you one helluva fight. And

206

if you don't kill me and you hurt our baby, I'm gonna kill you. Considering how you look, I might succeed."

Tre Pound stared into her defiant eyes. He was supposed to be angry at her, but he was actually just glad to be near her and not around a bunch of niggas in orange jumpsuits. She smelled fresh and was somehow more beautiful to look at. Her neck looked warm, and he swore he could see it pulsing with fervor. Frankly, he didn't know if he wanted to strangle her or fuck her again. He sort of wanted to do both—and these ambivalent feelings for her were getting harder and harder to maintain.

"What are you looking at?" she said, snappy. She gave her neck a little twist, adding attitude. "Put yo hands on me and see what happens."

Tre Pound's phone rang. He answered it while still standing in front of Camille, but he had to look away from her.

"Hello?"

"It's me. Tre Pound." It was Seneca, but he spoke as if he was introducing himself as Tre Pound. *It's me. Tre Pound.*

Tre Pound didn't know how to address him. He wished he wouldn't have gave Seneca his chain. Seneca took what he said literally. "What do you want ... Tre Pound."

"Detectives just came by the house," said Seneca. "They were looking for Camille."

His voice even sounded deeper. *Was he trying to sound like me too?* Tre Pound wondered.

Tre Pound looked at Camille, then asked Seneca, "What'd they want?"

"They wanted to talk to her, asking me and Momma where she was."

"Did they say why they were looking for her?"

"Yeah. They said you raped her and they wanted a statement from her. What were they talking about?"

"They're just making up shit, trying to charge me with all kinds of shit to get me off the streets."

"I thought so."

"What did yo momma say?"

"She told the detectives they need to stop worrying about you and Camille fucking each other and focus on who killed her sons. She's really torn up about it. I told her it was probably those 12th Street niggas that did it. She wants me and you to find them."

"I gotta go. I don't wanna be on the phone no longer than I have to."

"Okay. Are you coming to the funerals? They're scheduled on—"

Tre Pound hung up. Before he could stuff the phone back in his pocket Camille wanted to know what was going on.

"What did Seneca say?" she asked. "I can see it in yo face something happened."

"Detectives were over Bernice's house looking for you."

Camille paused. "That fast? They found Buttercup?"

"No. This is about that second charge they hit me with. They wanna ask me questions about me raping you."

"What the fuck?" Camille's face was scrunched up. "That was what they charged you with? Why didn't you tell me?"

"I'm telling you now. FBI recorded us having sex in my car and they also got me on tape telling you that Shelton killed Drought Man."

"Oh shit!"

"Yeah, that's right. And I'm blaming that shit on you."

"Me?"

"If you would've never tried to sneak outta town with Lil' Pat, none of that shit would've been recorded because it wouldn't have happened."

"Fuck you, Tre Pound."

"No, fuck you."

"They'll drop the charges on you because I won't cooperate," Camille said.

"If they obtained that tape legally, they're not gonna drop shit, whether you cooperate or not. They're gonna take me to trial."

"Well, that's even more reason for us to get the hell outta here."

"No, that's why we need to stay. I'm not going nowhere with my reputation hanging in the balance like that. If I run, I look guilty. I gotta beat these cases, especially the rape. I can't let that shit sit out there."

Tre Pound grabbed his crutches, positioning them under his arms. Once he felt supported, he crutch-walked toward the door.

"Where are you going?" Camille asked.

"To get some blunts."

"Can I go?"

"No. You need to look up some abortion clinics, unless you wanna see me go to jail."

She sucked her teeth, as he hobbled out the door.

Chapter 32

They had been at the Econo Lodge for almost a week now. Tre Pound only had two blunts worth of weed left, and he wasn't up for going out and taking more. He was feeling better, had been doing push-ups and squats and dips off the bed, but he knew he wasn't in good enough shape to try to pull off a weed robbery.

And that was disappointing. The weed had taken his mind off of things.

He hadn't asked Camille again about the abortion. He was sort of accepting that she wouldn't do it. *Accepting,* but not agreeing. They continued to play cards together for days like everything was fine, not speaking on murder or sex or prison, just pretending that I Declare War and Go Fish were the funnest games on earth.

"You stole my joker!" Camille laughed once, not even twenty minutes after she'd vomited in the toilet from pregnancy sickness. "You freakin' suck, Tre."

"Last game you stole my joker," Tre Pound said, smiling back at her. "It's my turn now, homie."

But behind their laughs and smiles there was still that underlying antagonism—would Tre Pound really kill her if she didn't get an abortion?

The Econo Lodge had an indoor pool. Tre Pound and Camille tested it out on their fourth day. They raced each other from one end of the pool to the other, Camille won all three times, and Tre Pound blamed it on his injuries.

"You can't blame it on that," she had said, treading the water in front of him. She grinned. "You're back to normal."

He had been standing in the water, tall enough to not have to tread. "My stomach is *still* hurting," he'd told her. "Give me a few more days and I'll beat you."

"You gotta realize I'm pregnant and I'm beating you. And in a few more days I'll be even more preg ..." Camille's words faltered when Tre Pound dove underwater and swam off.

She had accidentally broken the silent treaty not to speak about their child.

The next day went fine. Camille had started working out with him, holding his legs down so he could do proper sit-ups. With each sit-up, Tre Pound rose and touched his elbows to his knees. He did as many as he could— sit up, elbow-knee touch; sit up, elbow-knee touch. Camille's knees were planted on his feet. She needed all her weight to keep him planted. Her body was almost in between his legs, an intimate position, and every time he rose and crunched, he came closer to her beautiful face. She smiled encouragingly. "Ten more, Tre Pound! Come on! Nine more. Good, eight more." As he finished up, the idea entered his mind that maybe she thought he was coming around and no longer cared about the baby she was carrying.

Oh, how she was wrong.

The sixth night cooped up in that hotel room, Camille had had enough of the silence. During a new game of I

Declare War she suddenly picked up the deck and splashed the cards in his face.

"What the fuck is wrong with you?!" Tre Pound snapped.

"I'm tired of this!" she screamed.

"Pick those cards up."

"No! You're gonna listen to me!" She was standing up, blocking the light from the television. There were tears sliding down her cheeks. "You're gonna do something bad to me. I feel it."

"No, I'm not, Camille. Sit back down. Let's finish our game."

"Listen to me, Tre Pound. I've been doing research. We're not the first cousins to fall in love with each other. There was this family from the House of Habsburg in the Roman days. They ruled by keeping their dynasty restricted to family only. That's what we can do as Kings."

"You done? Can we finish playing now?"

"No." She wiped her tears with her palms and continued. "All throughout history people like us have existed. It's not our fault. It's not your fault or my fault; it's what is. Look me in my face and tell me you're not in love with me."

He looked at her, and was prepared to tell her those very words. But it wasn't the truth. He had actually come to grips with it before they had sex on the side of the highway, but kept trying to deny it. He didn't know when it had grown to this level, but it had. The sex they had was inevitable. It could have happened anywhere, at any time. He knew it. And she knew it. Thoughts of her had encompassed him for a very long time, so much so that he couldn't remember having a full week where he didn't dream about her.

He lowered his head, knowing he was going to regret what he was about to say.

He closed his eyes and took a deep breath. Then he opened them and stared at her once more. "I am in love with you," he said.

Camille gasped, and then she suddenly burst into tears, crying into her palms.

"But that still don't change shit," he added.

She looked up from her hands with red, teary eyes. "Yes, it does, Tre Pound. You don't even realize it."

"Can we finish our game?" he asked. "Please? I don't wanna talk about that shit. Not right now anyway. I got enough on my mind already."

Camille nodded, then started picking up the cards she had thrown in his face. She sat back down on his bed with him and began shuffling.

***

It was five minutes til midnight when Tre Pound's phone rang. He clicked on the lamp, washing the room in a soft light. It woke up Camille. She was in her bed rubbing her eyes as he put the phone up to his ear.

"Hello?"

"Mr. King, how are you?" asked Mr. Schnoll.

"I'm fine. Wussup?" Tre Pound tried not to sound nervous, but he was. A middle-of-the-night call from your lawyer couldn't be good.

"Bad news."

"I figured as much."

"You've just been issued another warrant for murder. I just got the word."

Tre Pound sat up. "What murder?" he asked, though he already had a pretty good clue.

"A woman by the name of Buttercup Williams was murdered several days ago. I'm afraid they're pinning it on you."

Tre Pound never knew her last name. He'd never cared.

"Witnesses at her job say that Buttercup was bragging to them that you were living with her. Same witnesses say Camille was living there too. And if I'm not mistaken, the address that was listed in the file is the same address where I dropped you off at after bonding you out. What have you gotten yourself into, Mr. King? Are you nuts?"

"Mr. Schnoll, I'm not saying I don't know her or that I didn't stay with her for a little bit. But I didn't kill that girl. I know nothing about it. This is the type of shit I was telling you about. The police are out to get me. They're trying to get all the Kings."

"You need to turn yourself in."

"When?"

"As soon as possible. Tomorrow."

"I've been watching the news faithfully for the last few days. What station did you see this on?"

"It wasn't on the news. Whenever I take on a client, I enter his or her name in a system, and that system is linked to a broader system that gives us lawyers access to judicial updates in real time. So whenever your name is entered into any database or document that's signed by a judge, I'm alerted. And yours was entered into a murder warrant sixteen hours ago. They're not gonna put this murder on the news. It was too gruesome, for one; and for two, you were linked to it. How would the city officials look if they broadcasted that you're a suspect in a young woman's murder and they *just* released you on bond for a double-cop murder and statutory rape charge? The public would have their heads on a stick. No, they're gonna protect their butts and capture you quietly. They're gonna keep this under wraps until you're apprehended. I'm telling you—you need to turn yourself in before they catch you."

Tre Pound thought about his uncle Cutthroat, how the police gunned him down during a traffic stop. Tre Pound knew that would be his fate if he didn't turn himself in.

Or leave Kansas City.

He told Miron Schnoll he'd call him first thing in the morning, then he hung up. He looked over at Camille, whose eyes were wide with shock. Obviously with how quiet the hotel room was she was able to hear the whole conversation.

"I won't let you go down for that," Camille said bravely. "I'll tell them it was me."

Tre Pound simply reached over and clicked off the lamp, and Camille's face disappeared in the darkness. Tre Pound laid back on his bed and sighed.

"You're not gonna turn yourself in tomorrow, are you?" Camille whispered in the dark. "They're not gonna let you bond out this time."

"I know."

"You can't leave me out here," she said.

"I know."

"We have to leave Kansas City. We have to go, Tre Pound, or they're gonna do you like they did my daddy."

"I know."

Chapter 33

The next morning Camille woke up before Tre Pound. She was folding her clothes on the dresser as quickly as she could, while Tre Pound sat up in his bed half sleep. He scooted back to the headboard so he could sit comfortably and watch Camille.

She ran to the bathroom and grabbed the shaving cream she'd left and stuffed that in the bag with her clothes. After a few seconds of looking around the room to see if she'd forgotten anything, she finally noticed that Tre Pound was awake.

"Good morning," she said with a smile. "How long have you been watching me?"

"Long enough to know that you need to slow yo ass down."

"I just don't wanna forget anything."

"Where's the duffel bag of money?"

Camille lifted it up by its strap with both hands. "Duffle bag, check. I got all your clothes packed too."

"We got this room till eleven. Sit down and relax."

"I can't." She went and sat down beside him, shivering with excitement. "Is this fa-real? Are we really leaving."

Tre Pound nodded. "We're outta here," he said, and

when Camille threw her arms around him to hug him, he shoved her off. "Camille, I got stabbed—"

"I know, I know. You're still sore. Sorry about that. I'm just so freaking happy!"

Unbeknownst to Camille, Tre Pound was having second thoughts. It had nothing to do with how excited Camille was, but instead how *unexcited* he was to leave his hometown. No one would know his name. No one would know he was Tre Pound.

He imagined all night what it would be like to be unknown. A regular joe with no enemies, no funk, no reason to carry a gun. It had some pluses. But throwing Camille in that equation, as well as a child—that's where things started to feel weird inside. Could they really make it work? He was in love with her—as unfathomable as that was, even to him sometimes—but did that make it right?

He'd just have to see.

He watched Camille brush her hair fast in the mirror, and her reflection smiled at him. He thought about her father, which was his uncle Cutthroat, and how he had a wife and a side chick and children with both women. Of course, Tre Pound's situation was completely different but he still found some solace in knowing he was on that same path, in his own way. Cutthroat wasn't born in Kansas City but he'd planted his roots here. Tre Pound could plant his own seeds somewhere new too.

His phone rang, and Camille's reflection frowned at him. She turned around to face him.

"Who is it?" she asked.

Tre Pound answered it. "Hello?"

Marlon Hayes said, "Who's gonna save you out here?"

"I don't need nobody to save me, nigga." Tre Pound got out of bed and pulled his pants on, then his shirt as quickly as he could. He grabbed his 9mm off the nightstand and went to the window and looked out the curtains. There was no way Marlon could know he was here but he had to be sure. He saw no one suspicious in the parking lot. "So they let yo bitch-ass out the county, huh?"

"I'm not gonna stop until you're dead, Tre Pound. So why don't you do us both a favor and let me kill you?"

"Let's do it."

"Do what?" Camille asked. She was standing behind Tre Pound, trying to hear the conversation.

He shoved her back angrily, then walked outside into the hallway to talk in private. His gun was in his front pocket, the handle sticking out.

"Let's do it," Tre Pound said into the phone again. "Let's get this shit over with. If you're ready to die, let's make it happen."

"How do I know you're not gonna call the police again?"

"The police are looking for me for another murder right now. Why would I call the police?"

"Put that on something. Put that on yo family's name you'll meet me somewhere and won't pull no ho shit."

"I'll meet you. I put that on King, I put that on my 'hood, it don't matter."

They agreed on a place to meet after Tre Pound insisted he pick the location. Marlon conceded and hung up before Tre Pound could ask what time. *I guess that means right now,* Tre Pound thought. He put his phone in his pocket and, while closing his hand on the knob to go back inside the hotel room, he wondered if what he was about to do was the right thing.

"Who was that?" Camille asked when he walked back in the room.

Tre Pound popped his clip out, checked to see if it was full, then popped it back in and stuck the gun in the back of his pants. "That was Marlon," he said, as he slipped into a T-shirt. "We're about to meet up."

"No, yall ain't," Camille said firmly. "We're leaving."

"Not until this is over."

"Tre Pound, that's too risky."

"Risky in what way? You're saying that you think he'll out-gun me? I was born with a gun in my hand!"

"Calm down. I'm saying it's risky because it increases the chances of you getting pulled over. We don't need to take that chance."

"I have to kill this nigga," Tre Pound said. "I can't leave after being called out by him. That man tried to kill me more than once, and Cash and Seneca. If I leave, the whole city will think I'm a bitch."

"Who cares?"

"I do, goddammit!" Tre Pound snapped.

"You're stalling because you really don't want to leave with me, aren't you?"

"If that's what you wanna believe." Tre Pound put on his shoes, laced them up so tight it sounded like they ripped. He stood up and got in Camille's face. "Marlon is obsessed with me. He got locked up on purpose just to try and kill me. All this shit is going on because he thinks I killed Dominique. He's fucked up in the head. I can let the other funk go, but not with him." He turned to grab his Porsche keys, but Camille grabbed his arm.

"I have to tell you something," she said.

"Tell me later."

"No! I have to tell you now."

"What, Camille?"

"I killed Dominique."

219

Tre Pound looked her in the eyes. This was the second time she'd said this to him. And like before, he answered, "No, you didn't. Young Ray killed her."

"He shot her, Tre Pound, but I killed her. It was right after I killed Young Ray. I ran over to Dominique and dragged her out of the car. She was barely conscious because she'd been shot. But she was still alive. I covered her nose and suffocated her. I held her down until she stopped shaking."

Tre Pound cocked his head, studying his little cousin from a new angle. If what she was saying was true ... "It makes no sense for you to do that," he stated, but it was almost a question.

"Dominique was trying to steal you," Camille cried. "She was talking about having your baby and being with you and I couldn't let it happen. I couldn't let her interfere with our love. I'll tell Marlon what I did and it won't be you that he's after."

Tre Pound slapped her and she went down to the floor hard. Her nose bled instantly. But Tre Pound wasn't done. He grabbed her by her hair as she tried to scramble away, then he steadied her head as best as he could and smacked her again.

"You killed her?! That's what you're telling me? This funk wit' Marlon is because of you?!"

Camille was disoriented. She crawled to the foot of her bed, tried to pull herself up but the sheets came sliding off and she fell back on the floor. She got tangled in them, and when Tre Pound tried to yank them away she held on.

"I'm sorry, Tre Pound! Stop, please!"

"What the fuck is wrong with you, Camille? Huh? You killed yo best friend?!"

"I did it for us!"

220

Tre Pound raised his hand again and she cowered away. He wanted to hit her at least one more time but there was already enough slick blood smeared under her nose and around her mouth, making her appear in worse shape than she was. Another smack and things could really get messy. He needed to let her clean herself up before housekeeping came knocking.

"Are we still leaving town?" she asked.

Chapter 34

Tre Pound hit the brakes so hard that Camille's head whipped forward. Her seatbelt caught her, but she looked at Tre Pound like he was the devil. Around the rim of her left nostril, blood had crusted.

"Get the fuck out my Porsche, killa." Tre Pound said it without smiling.

Camille looked to her right, outside her tinted window. The house she grew up in was glaring back at her threateningly. She hadn't been here since her mother was murdered in the basement.

"Can you drop me off somewhere else?" Camille asked.

"Nope."

"Why here?"

"You got keys to another house?"

She sucked her teeth. "My momma died here, Tre Pound. I'm scared to go in there by myself."

"Killers don't get scared," he said.

With an attitude, Camille threw off her seatbelt and opened her door. "Are you coming back?"

"I shouldn't. I wouldn't be wrong if I didn't. I can't believe I gotta go knock a nigga I once called my brother because of some shit you did."

"I said I'll call him and tell him that I did it."

"Or you can quit putting weight on my leather seat and raise up out. GET THE FUCK OUT MY CAR!'"

Camille got out and slammed the door. Tre Pound zoomed off before she could even see if her door key worked, and she could still hear the Porsche's sports-exhaust system long after the car disappeared out of sight.

She was mad at Tre Pound, but there was still a loving thought on her mind: *God, please let him make it back alive.*

The wood beneath her creaked when she walked in. She didn't remember the entrance making that sound before, but that could probably be because this house had never been this quiet when lived in. She stayed several feet away from the basement door as she passed it, too afraid it might burst open if she got too close and gnarled dead-body hands—thousands of them—would drag her down to the depths of hell.

I've watched too many horror movies to know that's how it works, she thought.

She jerked her head to the left when she heard a sound. It came from the kitchen. Lightly, she walked to the doorway and peeked in. She thought she saw something in the corner move, but the shadows were so thick and the movement so petty she couldn't be sure if she'd seen anything at all.

I'm being jumpy for nothing, she thought. *There's nothing in this house but me.* Yet, even after that reassuring thought, her heartrate seemed to beat faster.

Her hand found the light on the wall. She flicked it and nothing happened. There was no electricity.

She stepped closer to the shadows, trying her hardest to make out the odd shape in the corner of her kitchen, and that's when it moved. And it moved *fast!* The man who'd been lying in wait sprang forward, causing Camille to scream like she never had in her life. The man lifted his assault rifle and knocked her in the head with the butt of it.

She was unconscious before she hit the kitchen floor.

***

When she came to, she was still on the kitchen floor. Her head was throbbing and she was almost sure she had a knot. She tried to bring her hand up to feel, but her arm wouldn't move. Neither one of her arms had leeway. Her hands were duct-taped behind her back!

She started to panic, squirming and breathing faster, and that's when she realized her mouth and legs were duct-taped too. And the way her jaws felt—sticky and restricted—it was apparent that her attacker had went all the way around her head with the tape at least three times.

"Where's Tre Pound?"

She couldn't see Marlon but she damn sure heard him. Struggling to get an arm loose, she only managed to strain her shoulder. And she really had to pee.

"Where is he? I searched through every fucking nook and cranny of this house. What trick is he trying to pull? Are you some kind of bait?"

How does he expect me to answer and my mouth is gagged? Camille thought.

She tried to figure out why this was happening to her. What was Marlon doing here? Was Tre Pound headed into a trap too? If so, why was Marlon looking around expecting Tre Pound to be here?

Marlon snatched off her duct-tape and she sucked in as much air as she could. He lifted her up and slung her over his shoulder and carried her upstairs. She didn't know what was about to happen to her, and she was too afraid to ask.

At the top of the stairs, he shrugged her off of his shoulder and draped her over the wood railing. He put a pistol to the back of her head, and Camille imagined that if he pulled the trigger, not only would her brains be blown out, but she'd tumble over the railing and fall at least forty feet to the floor below.

"Tell him to come out or I'ma shoot you," Marlon said. "I don't care about your life so you better say it like you mean it."

"He's not here!" Camille screamed. Teetering over this railing was causing blood to rush to her head. "He went to go meet you at the location yall picked."

"This *is* the location we picked."

Camille's heart skipped a beat. If where Marlon and Tre Pound were supposed to meet was in fact here, at her mother's house, then that meant Tre Pound dropped her off to be murdered.

She'd been set up!

She didn't know if it was the cutting betrayal or the influx of blood to her head that was suddenly making her dizzy. Nonetheless, she was having trouble keeping her eyes open.

Marlon snatched her off the railing and threw her against the wall. He pressed the muzzle of his gun to her forehead. He had his assault rifle strapped to his back.

"Talk," he said.

Camille was crying. She had to gather herself to form words. "Tre Pound ... isn't here. He left me here. He wants you to kill me ... because he can't do it himself."

"I believe Tre Pound is capable of that, but he wouldn't do that to you."

"Well, he did. I'm here, and you're gonna kill me because he's not coming back."

"He just dropped you off and left? That was him in that new Porsche?"

"Yes."

"Son of a bitch! That coward!" Marlon's jaws clenched. "Why does that pussy muthafucka want you dead?"

"Because ..." She swallowed. "Because I'm the reason yall are funking."

"It has nothing to do with you, Camille. And he knows that. I want him dead because his funk got Dominique killed. She should have never been in his car."

"I was part of the reason Dominique was in that car. I wanted to get Tre Pound some gizzards while he was in the hospital just as much as she did. I couldn't drive because I don't have a license." She paused to catch her breath. "Once we got back to the hospital, Young Ray cut us off in the parking garage and he shot Dominique but he didn't kill her. I finished her off. I killed Dominique. She would have lived if I didn't suffocate her."

Looking up at Marlon, she noticed how scraggly his beard was. His eyes were red and worn down, and his breath wasn't pleasant at all. He looked and smelled like a monster, a sharp contrast from the handsome man he used to be.

She noticed he wasn't pointing the gun at her anymore. He was staring back at her as if he was deciding what to do with her. A tear fell from his eye, and his lips started to tremble.

Then he pulled out a switchblade.

***

Once Tre Pound shifted into fifth gear, he was able to coast down the highway. He was listening to a song called "Been Thru It All" by a southern rapper named Yo Gotti. The lyrics spoke of a man going through countless life-threatening situations and making it out on top. The song sort of matched what Tre Pound was feeling right now, except for the fact that he hadn't made it out the streets yet.

He could, though, if he just kept driving.

The Porsche's engine got louder, a warning sign that the RPMs were too high and Tre Pound either needed to speed up or downshift into fourth gear. He had slowed down unconsciously, because deep down he didn't want to leave Kansas City.

He downshifted into fourth.

Cooped up in that hotel room, alone with Camille for so many days, had ruined him. He had enjoyed her company so much that he had confessed that he was in love with her, something he swore he would never do. Then, to make matters worse, he found himself envisioning a life with her and their child. Crazy! How could that have ever worked?

When Camille revealed that she killed Dominique, when Tre Pound accepted it as truth, that was when he knew without a shadow of a doubt that Camille was toxic. She needed to be murdered for the sake of the family name, for the sake of Tre Pound's reputation. If she were to live, there was no telling what damage she could do.

But as much as Tre Pound tried to convince himself that he did the right thing by setting Camille up, he felt like shit inside. He missed Camille already. He missed Kansas City, and he wasn't even outside the city limits yet.

He downshifted into third, then merged into the far right lane. The slow lane. Then he found himself pulling all the way to the side of the road. He slowed down and the Porsche engine purred, as if it didn't want to stop. Tre Pound parked on the shoulder of the highway and cut the car off.

He wondered how Marlon would kill her—would he shoot her, stab her, beat her to death or torture her? If it was Tre Pound, he would choose torture. Maybe throw her down the steps with enough force to snap her wrist and then pistol-whip her bloody until she told him what he wanted to hear. Then he'd cut her throat.

Tre Pound remembered slicing Latrice across her jugular and standing there patiently as she bled out, then shooting her girlfriend Joy in the back and watching her tumble down the basement steps. It was a lot of steps too, making the fall almost comical.

Camille didn't deserve to die that way.

And now Tre Pound was starting to regret dropping her off.

"You did what you had to do," he said to himself out loud. "Don't bitch-up now. A hard decision had to be made. You did the right thing, Tre Pound."

But even his own words couldn't console him. He suddenly felt a rush of uncontrollable anger at the thought of Marlon having his way with a King. So much pressure was building up inside, his eyes started to water.

"You better not cry. Bitch-ass nigga, if you cry, that makes you soft. You're not soft, are you?" He squeezed his eyes shut, but that only made a tear fall. "Man-up, nigga. Shake this shit off. Shake it off, Tre Pound. You're acting like a pussy fa-real."

He opened his eyes and took a deep breath, and that's when a wave of tears started to fall. He was crying, something he hadn't done since he made love to Camille that night. He stared at the high-end luxury of his dashboard, not knowing or caring what half of the buttons did, focusing more on how hot the tears felt as they poured down his cheeks, then dwelling on how desperately he wanted to be near Camille right now. He wanted to be inside her, to tell her he was sorry, to tell her again that he was in love with her. He wanted to scream it at her, make her feel it.

Against his better judgment, he started the Porsche back up, shifted into gear and took off in a cloud of dust toward the first exit. As he gripped the leather steering wheel, he kept thinking, *I hope I'm not too late, I hope I'm not too late ...*

Chapter 35

Camille closed her eyes tight and held her breath as she waited for the switchblade to penetrate her. She heard the near-silent *swipe* of it, and both her arms suddenly felt lighter, but she didn't feel the pain. The blade must have gone through her skin so fast that the feeling was delayed. She clenched her teeth together, preparing for the onslaught of flesh-splitting pain, when there was another *swipe* and her legs suddenly felt loose and wobbly.

She was about to pass out.

"Breathe," Marlon said.

She did, sucking in air so fast she started coughing. She looked at him and then the knife—there was no blood on it. It was then that she noticed her hands weren't bound, neither were her legs. He had cut her free.

"Why did you kill my sister?" Marlon asked. "Did Tre Pound make you?"

Camille hesitated. "No. He didn't know I did it until today. That's probably part of the reason he left me here," she said. Marlon still had the switchblade out. She continued, even though death was sure to be the outcome. Marlon deserved to know. "I killed her because I thought she was taking Tre Pound away from me. She was talking about having his baby, starting a family with him, and I couldn't take it. So you need to kill me and not Tre Pound. It wasn't his fault. It was mines."

Marlon's eyes were full of tears. He looked like he was on the brink of going insane. "Make me understand, Camille. Please? Why would you think my sister was capable of 'stealing' Tre Pound from you?"

"She was doing it whether she realized it or not. He was spending more time with her than he did with me. He bought me some gifts once, then turned around and gave them to her. He was starting to care about her more than me."

"He cared about Dominique?"

"Yes."

"Did Tre Pound love her?"

"I don't know. I didn't want him to."

"You only wanted him to love you?"

Camille nodded. "I'm in love with him," she confessed.

Marlon narrowed his eyes at her in a way that made her feel judged. "You need help," he said.

"Maybe I do. But I can't help how I feel or take back what I've done."

"You have the same fire as Dominique."

"No, I don't. I'm nothing like her."

"Where are you gonna go if I let you go?"

Camille blinked. She hadn't thought about being let go; she was so positive he was going to kill her. And suddenly the thought of being alive, without Tre Pound, seemed worse than dying. She started sobbing into her hands, the duct-tape still dangling from her wrists.

"I have nowhere to go!" she wailed.

"You can come with me," Marlon said.

She kept crying. "Just kill me!"

"I won't do it, Camille. You've suffered enough. Your mother is gone, your big brother is incarcerated, two of your brothers were killed days ago, and your cousin just abandoned you." He grabbed her wrists gently. "Come with me."

She opened her eyes, staring Marlon directly in the face. She could see all the pain he was going through. All the pain she caused. The way he was holding her wrists, which was growing tighter, revealed how much he needed her.

Did he expect her to live with him, as if she was his new little sister? Did he want her to take Dominique's place? Camille wondered if she could do it, if she could live that lie.

Marlon squeezed her wrists until they hurt. "Come with me!"

Camille felt compelled to say yes, but then she cut her eyes to the right and caught sight of Tre Pound mounting the staircase quietly. She gasped, and Marlon turned a second too late.

Tre Pound lifted his handgun and fired once. His shot hit home—the side of Marlon's skull exploded and the velocity slammed his head into the wall. He laid to rest beside Camille, shuddering once before taking his last breath.

Tre Pound shot him twice more.

Camille flinched each time. She was covered in blood now. She stared at it running down her palms, then looked up at Tre Pound, who was holding the murder weapon at his side. He looked at her with severe apology.

"I'm sorry," he said.

"Sorry?" she questioned.

"I couldn't let him do it."

Camille used the wall to help herself to her feet, leaving bloody handprints on the paint. With unsteady legs, she ran at Tre Pound and punched him repeatedly.

"You're sorry?!" she screamed. She was striking him as hard as she could, and he wasn't trying hard at all to fend her off. "Fuck you, Tre Pound! I hate you!"

"You *should* hate me."

"You know I don't hate you! But I want to kill you!"

"I'm sorry."

Camille punched until she tired herself out. Then Tre Pound hugged her to his chest and let her cry. She felt a few tears of his drop on the top of her head. After a moment, she looked up into his eyes.

"I'm mad that I still love—" she began.

He kissed her lips, absorbing the rest of her words. Camille didn't know what was going on but she didn't stop him. His lips felt too good. She wrapped her arms around his neck, and when he squeezed her butt—almost painfully—she jumped up and wrapped her legs around him.

"Don't leave me again," she moaned as he sucked on her bottom lip.

"I'm in love with you, Camille." He licked and kissed her neck, her chin, then her mouth again. "I'm in love with you."

"I'm in love with you, too. But don't leave me again. Please, Tre Pound, don't leave me."

Tre Pound laid her down right there on the carpet, in the hallway, eight feet away from Marlon's body. Camille unbuttoned her jeans and he yanked them off in one pull. She saw something in his eyes that she didn't like, but she ignored it. She just wanted him inside her.

"Fuck me," she said, lifting her legs in the air so he could have her panties. He tossed them over his shoulder and they went over the rail, floating merrily downstairs. He pushed his pants down and Camille felt that same lovely fear she'd felt the first time she saw his dick.

She clenched her teeth as he entered her. Once he filled her up and her fleshy walls could expand no more, she squealed, "Mercy!" and he eased back.

But only to thrust back in even deeper.

She lost her breath.

Tre Pound hollered, "I'm in love with you!"

They were holding each other tight as they humped in disorderly motions, both of them trying to outfuck the other. Camille's eyes were closed, her lips slightly parted, and a breathy moan escaped her lips that came from the wonderful hotness her pussy was experiencing.

This is better than before! she thought, as she climaxed and he continued to overpower her. *I need air. Oh my God, he's so strong.*

"Tre Pound ... chill, baby. Let's leave."

He'd risen to his knees, and he was gripping her by the waist and slamming himself into her. "Not till I cum ..."

"Hurry up."

When he turned her over and began fucking her from the back, suddenly she was no longer in a rush; at least not as much. He was flattening her booty with so much force, she could think of nothing else but, "Keep going, Tre, just keep going. Dammit, man!" She came again, a waterfall of juices soaking his shaft and seeping down her inner thighs. She started biting the top of her thumb so hard it left an indent.

She glanced over at Marlon's body, wincing at how twisted his neck looked. And just when the idea of murder began to work its way in her mind and through her forcefield of pleasure, Tre Pound yanked her hair and pounded into her harder, and that tiny spark of remorse evaporated in a snap.

She licked her lips, tasting blood that wasn't her own and she didn't even notice.

Tre Pound snatched her head back further, forcing her upright on her knees, just like he was. From behind, he continued to fuck her, and when his arm went around her neck and his other hand squeezed between her thighs, she thought it was all a part of his gift of love-making.

Until his arm tightened too quick and her throat sent a distress signal to her brain.

"Tre, I can't breathe!"

It didn't come out as loud as she wanted it to. She tried to utter it again and couldn't even roll out half a sentence. His arm had gotten even tighter—and then paralyzingly tight!

Oh my God!

His fingers dug deeper into her pussy. "I'm in love with you," he croaked.

This time, the way he said it was clear to her. It wasn't endearing; it was malicious. He was telling her he was in love with her as if it was something he despised, something he couldn't live with.

Camille panicked. "Tre, no!"

But he didn't let up. She could feel his powerful muscles constricting even more, so much so that she was sure her bones would shatter before she suffocated. She remembered he had a weak spot—his stomach. But the minute she tried to find it, her instinct told her to keep pulling on his arms for air.

"I couldn't let Marlon do it," he whispered. "I had to do it myself. I'm sorry."

Camille was starting to black out, and she knew that she would be dead soon. Just before her eyes fluttered shut and she sunk into the abyss of death, she felt him cumming inside of her.

It was the worst feeling she ever felt.

Chapter 36

4 months later

Tre Pound was back in the county jail in an orange jumpsuit, which was a lot better than the alternative—fleeing Kansas City with his pregnant 15-year-old cousin and attempting to start a new life with her. He wasn't proud of what he had to do to get here, but he was content in knowing that he made a decision based on logic and not his heart.

He had manned-up.

The buttons on his jumper were crooked, so he re-buttoned them as he waited for the guard to receive clearance through the visiting room door. It buzzed, the guard tugged it open, and Tre Pound walked in with a professional smile.

He shook Miron Schnoll's hand, then had a seat.

"Are you ready?" asked Mr. Schnoll.

"Ready as I'll ever be."

"I'ma have to ask you again to rethink this."

"I thought it through enough. I just wanna plead guilty and do my time."

"This isn't the best deal we can get, Mr. King."

"I know."

Miron Schnoll fixed him with a stern look. "Okay, just so we're clear, I wanna go over everything one more time. I don't wanna get in that courtroom and you find out that this isn't what you want. The prosecutor is expecting us to plead out today." Miron looked down at his document. "You're agreeing to plead guilty to the murder of Buttercup Williams. In exchange for this guilty plea, the double cop murders will be dropped, and so will the statutory rape charges. Does this sound right?"

"Yes, sir."

"And you know the murder charge you want to plead guilty to carries a heftier sentence than the rape charge, right?"

"I don't care."

Miron sighed. "Mr. King, the Buttercup Williams charge is voluntary manslaughter, a Class B felony in the state of Missouri. It holds a maximum penalty of 15 years. On the other hand, the statutory rape charge is a class C and only holds a maximum of 7 years. I'm guaranteeing you that I can beat the cop murders as well as the Buttercup Williams murder. And if it wasn't for that recording, I could guarantee the rape case too. But even with all that's stacked against us, I can get you better than 15 years. Let me do my job."

"Your job is to get the deal I want. And if taking a murder rap will get rid of that rape shit, that's what I wanna do."

Miron Schnoll didn't seem to comprehend taking more time than you had to. But it wasn't his job to understand.

Tre Pound had thought it all the way out. Pleading guilty to Buttercup's murder would make him even more revered in the streets. He could spin it as a revenge kill— Buttercup stabbed him in the hand and shoulder outside the restaurant she worked at, so Tre Pound came back later on and murdered her in her own home. He would have pleaded guilty to the cop murders too—'hood niggas would have praised him for generations for that, especially since his uncle was gunned down by a traffic cop—but the penalty was too stiff. For two dead police officers, he'd have to take a life sentence.

No way, José.

He would take the blame for the Buttercup murder, ensuring that his name would be cleared in the statutory rape of his little cousin, and he'd be able to do his time with his reputation intact. By the time he was released he'd be a legend in Kansas City, and still young enough to take over the city once again.

As he listened to his lawyer sit across from him and explain the process of a guilty plea and the rights he'd have to waive, his mind wandered to where he'd buried Camille. He was pretty sure they would never find her body, and hopefully by the time they did, no evidence would be able to be lifted from her remains. He hated to picture a girl as beautiful as Camille reduced to bones, but that was the reality. That was what he'd have to live with.

"Are you listening?" Mr. Schnoll asked. "Why are you smiling?"

"I'm just proud to be a King ... that's all. I love being Tre Pound. Go ahead, continue."

***

Tre Pound sat down on the stand and shrugged the lapels of his jumper so he looked presentable. He raised his right hand and swore to tell the truth, and he did the exact opposite as he explained to the judge and prosecutor how he murdered Buttercup with a shard from a broken vase. It was the funniest thing, he thought, pleading guilty to a crime he didn't do. Out of all the crimes he'd committed—and he was responsible for some heinous ones—they were convicting him of one he had no involvement in.

After the plea process was all over and he was walking off the stand, Mr. Schnoll patted him on his back and told him to call him when he got back to his module. Since there was no trial, Miron owed Tre Pound some of his money back. Tre Pound told him to send it to him in increments every quarter.

On the shuttle bus back to the county jail, Tre Pound thought about his big cousin Shelton. He had heard that Shelton got thirty years Fed time. If that was true, he wouldn't be coming home till he was sixty years old, or close to it. Tre Pound felt bad about it, but there was nothing he could do. What Tre Pound told Gutta in confidence and Camille in private—which happened to be recorded—shouldn't be held against him. And if Shelton did hold it against him, fuck him.

Tre Pound was still able to walk back in his module with his head held high.

"My nigga Tre Pound is back! How much time did we get?" It was said by Tyrell Sipple, as he gave Tre Pound dap, welcoming him back into the module. Tyrell was wearing a shirt tied around his head as a du-rag. He had told Tre Pound he helped beat the shit out of Marlon Hayes for no other reason than Marlon had it coming.

Tre Pound respected him for that.

"I won't know how much time I get until sentencing," Tre Pound said to Tyrell. "But they can't give me any more than fifteen."

"Congrats!"

"Thank you."

"I put today's *Kansas City Star* on yo bed. Yo cousin Shelton is on the front page, and you're mentioned in the article too."

"A'ight. Good lookin' out."

Tre Pound was so in a hurry to get to his cell he hopped over the bottom tier railing and landed right in front of his door. He scooped up the newspaper off his bed and shook it straight.

On the front page, there was an old photo of Shelton being escorted out of King Financial by the FBI. His face was captured in a squint, as if the camera flashes were blinding him. To the public it would probably look like he was frowning. But Shelton wasn't a person who frowned. This picture was an attempt to portray him as a mean person.

The headline of the article—KANSAS CITY MAN PUTS THE KING IN KINGPIN.

Tre Pound laughed out loud, then started reading:

A federal judge handed out a 30-year term to a Kansas City resident named Shelton King last Wednesday. In his indictment it stated that he ran a criminal enterprise out of his loan business, King Financial, since day one of the company's grand opening. Money laundering, extortion, and bribery was said to take place behind its doors as if it were everyday business. Employees there seemed to have no knowledge of their boss's criminal activity. His vice president, Kimberly Washington, had this to say: " Mr. Shelton King is an honest business man. These charges are bullcrap, and it goes to show how bloodthirsty our nation's prosecutors are." Since Mr. King's conviction, Ms. Kimberly Washington hasn't been available for comment.

In addition to the above crimes, Mr. King was convicted of the cold-case murder of Derrick "Drought Man" Weber. Federal officials said Shelton King's decision to murder Derrick was based on " the economy of the local drug market" —in other words, dead drug dealers meant big business for King Financial. Overwhelming evidence obtained from confidential informants, wire taps, and good old-fashioned police work helped to solidify a conviction.

Tre Pound was prompted to turn to page 3 to finish the article. He did, and he was stunned by how much more of the story was left. Thomas Lackman, the writer of the article, took it all the way back to the 70s, the era in which Marcus "Cutthroat" King ran Kansas City. Thomas started from Cutthroat's membership in the Black Liberation Army and went into his participation in robbing local and out-of-town drug dealers. A brief story on Shelton's rumored life as a drug kingpin came next, and in the same paragraph Maurice "Gutta" King was called Shelton's "enforcer." Nowhere did it mention that Gutta was a confidential informant, only that he and his little brother were murdered and their killer(s) was still at large.

Without even realizing it, Tre Pound said out loud, "Camille would've love to read this article." And as he kept reading, he finally came across his own name. They had saved the best for last.

21-year-old Levour King, otherwise known as Tre Pound, is Shelton King's younger cousin— some say protégé—and he is facing a murder charge of his own and is expected to plead guilty to it by the end of the week. Levour King is described by his peers as ruthless, villainous, pugnacious, backstabbing, and downright evil. It's a wonder that police officials have been wanting to take him off the streets way before he reached drinking age. Dynisha Miller, a woman who testified against him in a previous murder case where he was found not guilty, claims he put her in a wheelchair in retaliation. She was once his friend, and she explains the madness behind the man. " He's from the Tre block," she says. "And it ain't nothing but troublemakers over there. He was raised in that environment. He also comes from a family of bad people. Everybody around here has heard some crazy story about the King family. But Tre Pound ... he's been killing people all his life. He's the worst King of 'em all. "

For now, the King family terror has ended, and the citizens of Kansas City can finally live in peace.

By the time Tre Pound finished the article, he had to start over and read it again. He was amazed by the accuracy of the writer. And nowhere in it was there anything about a rape.

Bravo, Mr. Thomas Lackman. I couldn't have written this story any better myself.

Chapter 37

Shavon Guy left her son strapped in his car seat, as she sat on the couch and rocked him with her bare foot. She was watching a rerun of *Martin: Season Two,* and was so lost in the on-screen antics that she didn't notice her son was coughing until the scene changed.

"Tyler!"

She unstrapped him, picked him up and draped him on her shoulder. "Breathe, little boy," she said, as she patted his back repeatedly. "Please, breathe."

The baby took a heaving lungful of air, coughed a few more times and finally started breathing normally.

"Thank you, Jesus."

She went from relief to anger in an instant, as she pinpointed the cause of her son's sudden fit. He hadn't started coughing like this until Spook started smoking his high-class weed in the house. The rank smell still lingered in the air, thick and suffocating.

"Spook!" she yelled.

He supposedly went upstairs to use the restroom, but he was probably up there on the phone with another bitch. She and Spook weren't together, but she birthed his son so that gave her first rights to his time and energy. She refused to be made a fool of. Everybody expected her to be this stupid teenaged mother who let a thug BD from 12th Street walk all over her, but she wasn't the one.

Not this Shavon Guy from Tre block.

Patting her son's back soothingly, she went upstairs and walked in the bathroom. The window above the tub was open, and the curtains fluttered like the dress of an unseen ghost. It gave her the creeps so she reached up and shut it.

A sound from behind startled her. She jerked her head around and saw nothing. "Spook?" she whispered.

No response.

Tyler hiccupped.

Then she heard a cry come from the attic. A man's cry. Spook's cry!

She started up the attic steps, thinking hard about that cry. It was the same sound Spook made during sex. The last thing she expected to find up here was Spook fucking some tackhead, but she couldn't put it past him. Since he'd been making beaucoup money with the drugs, he'd been getting beside himself. She had found a condom in Tyler's diaper bag.

"Hurry the fuck up, nigga!"

Shavon froze. That wasn't Spook's voice, but it sounded awfully familiar. She took another step up, and she was just the right height to be eye-level with the attic floor. A couple feet away she saw Seneca King, a boy she used to go to school with—whose brother she once dated—standing over her baby daddy with a gun that looked too heavy for Seneca to hold. The 3-foot fireproof safe, which had an electronic keypad and a tri-spoke handle, was already open.

"I said hurry up!" Seneca smacked her son's father
with the pistol. "I want everything in there, muthafucka.
The cocaine too."

"You ain't built for this shit, lil' nigga," Spook said
to him, as he stuffed the duffle bag with vacuum-sealed
bricks of cocaine. "Seneca, you're trying to be somebody
you're not."

"I told you my name's not Seneca. It's Tre Pound. I'm
holding it down until the original Tre Pound comes home.
You better respect it."

"You don't wanna take on his name out here, I'm
telling you. Stay in school, lil' nigga. His funk—"

Seneca pistol-whipped him again, opened up a nasty
gash right on the top of her man's black bald head. Spook
was hardly thrown off by the blow, though he was bleeding
pretty bad. He kept stuffing the duffle bag routinely, as if
he'd been through something like this before. He pulled
everything out of the safe, a safe Shavon didn't even have
a combination to—and this was her house. She sort of felt
like her baby daddy deserved this treatment.

Tyler started to stir. Shavon didn't want to be discovered
so she tiptoed back down the steps, all the way back down
to her seat on the couch, where she placed Tyler beside
her on his stomach. She was patting his back and looking
at Martin Lawrence on the TV absentmindedly, thinking
about what was happening right above her head.

She was scared, but also didn't know what the fuck to
do. Spook had told her the robbery game would be over
once Tre Pound got convicted, but that was a lie because
now Seneca was up there taking his place. Now Spook
would be out in the streets at crazy hours of the night
again, trying to hustle his money back until he found and

murdered Seneca. And then what if Spook found him? Would he get away with the murder? Who knows. Shavon just wanted him to spend more time with her and their son.

The bullshit never ends, Shavon thought.

She picked up the remote and pointed it at the TV, clicking the volume up a few notches. Before long, she found herself laughing at the screen, and for that moment in time the street life wasn't her reality.

LOVE/HATE LETTERS

The following are the lost letters between Moses Walker and Krystal Hamilton. They never received their letters, but through sheer happenstance they have been compiled here in chronological order.

~

Dear Krystal aka My Queen,

Worst day of my life when I found out you got locked up in juvenile detention. You got caught up in Shelton's shit and it broke my fucking heart. I love you, and I hate to see you in the same box I'm in.

I know you're having trouble adjusting to prison life so I'm taking the time to guide you through with a few tips. Rule #1: No friends. None of them bitches in there with you are your friends. Don't let people "buddy hustle" you. They'll try to be your friend just to borrow from you and get shit for free. Rule #2: Read. They have tons of books here in the Feds so I assume they would have just as many in the juvenile system. Read as much as you can. It occupies the mind. Because if you don't occupy it with something positive, then negative thoughts will weave their way in your brain. You don't want that, Krystal. Intermix fiction and nonfiction. For every three fiction books you read, pick up a nonfiction one. It's healthy. Rule #3: Exercise. You're gonna need your strength in there for when suckas try you. You wanna be at your best physical health in there. Even if one of the girls can fight better than you, you can still win if you have better wind and stamina.

Okay, I'ma stop right here for now. I don't wanna give you all my ancient Chinese secrets in one letter. Lol! Write me back and let me know what problems you have and I'll give you the answers. I love you, Krystal.

Love, *Moses*

~

Dear Moses,

I'm patiently waiting on your first letter. I really need to hear from you. It's like hell in here! Everybody's so mean. Well, not everybody. I've made a few friends that seem like nice girls. They're nice sometimes anyway, but that's life, right? This girl named Tangie White is real cool. She gave me her cereal my first day here! How real is that? I know you're big on "real," so that's the type of people I try to hang around. I miss you so much.

I think it's cool that Camille is willing to send our letters out. She's going out of her way to make sure we can connect so I'm gonna make a Thank You card for her. I'm making a card for you too, baby. I guess I'm gonna stop here before I start writing about my problems, plus Tangie needs to borrow my pen. Until next time baby. Muah!

Love, *Krystal*

~

Dear Wifey,

I haven't got your letter yet, but I'm writing again before I forget my thoughts. I've had a lot of time to think in here and I've realized that you're the girl of my dreams. I've never had anybody hold me down like you have. In the beginning I thought you were just some pretty young girl who loved the dick, but then I found out that you really care about me.

I'm saying this to say that I have big plans for us. I'm talking wedding bells and bad ass kids. I'm not just running game either. That's what most people assume— oh, he's locked up he wants to marry you now. No, I'm real. And you know I'm all about being real. So you know it's genuine when I say I can see you as my wife. Do you think I'm husband material? Can you see me in a robe with a tobacco pipe, reading the morning paper? I think I can be about that life. I can change. But only for you, Krystal.

I'm going to hold off on writing again until I know you're receiving my letters. I love you with everything I have in me. Know that as fact. And don't let nobody tell you different. It's Moses and Krystal against the world.

Always and Forever, *Moses*

~

Dear Moses,

It's a couple reasons I haven't wrote you yet. I didn't
have any stamps for a while. I told Tangie she could have
one stamp and she took THEM ALL. Lol! It was just a
miscommunication. The other reason I haven't wrote is
because I was waiting on your letter, but I just found out
why I haven't received it. Camille hasn't been able to mail
our letters off because she's been moving. I hope you've
called her and got the new address.

I hate this place, Moses. I feel like a slave. I have to
work for free and shower in public and get pushed around,
and if I fight back I get sent to the hole. I've never been
to the hole and I don't want to find out what it's like. So
I'm doing everything I can to stay out of there. I'll sure be
glad when I get your letter you talked about on the phone
where you mentioned jail tips. I need all the pointers I can
get because I feel like I'm doing this all wrong.

I love you.

Love, *Krystal*

~

Krystal,

What the fuck is going on? Is Camille not sending the letters off or are you not writing me back? I've never known Camille not to stick by her word, but I'm not too sure about you. It makes me wonder if you're already out of juvenile and you're out there fucking a bunch of off-brand niggas. You probably couldn't wait till I got locked up so you could go on a fuckfest. I thought you was a real one. Thought wrong, huh? I should've listened to these niggas in here when they told me writing you won't amount to shit. You proved them right. Bitches ain't shit.

How much you wanna bet I don't send you another letter?

One Hunnit, Moses aka A Real Nigga

~

Dear Moses,

Hey, I still haven't received your letter but I have faith I will. That's what's been keeping me going, faith in knowing I'll get to read your beautiful words.

I have some bad news and some good news. The bad news is I got into a fight with Tangie. She got mad because I hid my stamps from her so she hit me in my face. The good news is I didn't go to the hole because I didn't fight her back. Her punches didn't hurt anyway. I think that means I'm getting tougher, like you wanted me to be. I've started doing push-ups too. You'd be so proud! I still hate it here but I feel like things have gotten better since Tangie has been gone. I met a girl named Johnna today. She said she would've told me Tangie was no good but she didn't want to seem like a hater. Johnna seems like a cool friend. She helps me with my work out, and only charges me a little bit of food a day to train me. I'm gonna be so cute and fit the next time you see me

I love you!

Love, Krystal

~

Bitch,

I don't even know why I'm writing you again. You're probably riding a dick right now, perfecting the craft of whoredom. I hope that dick is equipped with AIDs, and yall pass it on to the bastard child yall make. And don't be trying to come running back to me when I get out of here and you see a nigga balling. I'ma just tell you to keep fucking the niggas you been fucking. I might let you suck my dick though, because I heard you can't catch AIDs by getting head. Just in case, I'm wearing a condom.

This is yo loss, not mine. I don't need you to write me or hold me down. I can find thousands of Krystals. Yo breed are a dime a dozen. But you'll never find another hustling nigga like me ever again in yo life. Trust me.

One Hunnit, Moses

~

Dear Moses,

I haven't been able to talk to Camille lately. Last time I talked to her she was living with a girl named Buttercup. She says she's gonna send off the letters, so all we can do is be patient. I hope you're not stressing out and thinking I'm not writing you. You know better than that :) I'm your ride or die forever.

Love, Krystal

~

Dear Krystal,

I've been letting this place get to me. The last couple letters I wrote were malicious and mean-spirited, and I'm sorry. It's hard going so long without hearing from you and I'm worried as fuck. My mind is fucking with me. It hasn't been looking good for me and my situation either. I just found out that Gutta, Tre Pound's cousin, is the informant on my case. My lawyer said I'm looking at 20 years if I don't cooperate. I'm not cooperating, so it is what it is. I don't blame you for not wanting to be in my corner. I have a lot of time to do and I don't wanna hold yo life up waiting on me. Go find you one of them good college muthafuckas. Them niggas is more yo speed anyway. I'd be pissed if you got with another thug nigga, but I'll respect whatever decision you make. I don't know how my life is gonna turn out, and I don't want you to get caught up in that uncertainty. Go live yo life, get you a good job and a good man and be happy. That's what it's all about—being happy.

This is my last letter. I gotta focus more on the inside than out there. It'll only distract me from jailing. I love you and I wish you the best.

Love, Moses

Chapter 38

Leavenworth, Kansas
United States Penitentiary (USP)

Moses took his shirt off and laid it down on the concrete floor as a makeshift mat. He flexed his muscles a little bit, did some overhead and downward stretches, then dropped down and started knocking out push-ups. As hard as he tried not to, he kept thinking about Krystal every time he pushed off the ground. She was probably the most beautiful girl he ever had, and that was no exaggeration. She had been the most loyal without a doubt.

He loved her.

But sometimes the one you love has to be let go, he told himself.

He hadn't wrote her a letter in over a year. Well, he'd wrote a couple recently but he hadn't sent any off to the last address Camille had given him in over a year.

With the image of Krystal's face on his mind, he managed to knock out a hundred push-ups straight. Grunting, he stood to his feet and took a sip from his bottled water.

"Looks like you got a little bigger since the last time I seen you," said one of the four inmates approaching Moses.

Moses pulled the bottle from his lips and capped it. He looked at all four men, but squinted at the man who'd spoken to him, not because he didn't recognize him but because he was almost in disbelief that they ended up at the same federal prison.

"Shelton! My nigga!" Moses gave him dap. "Good to see you. Good to see somebody I know from the streets. It's not a lot of Kansas City niggas in here."

"I heard they hit you with twenty."

"Yep. I read in the paper that you got thirty."

Shelton nodded, didn't seem fazed by the time. "That's how my cards fell, for now."

"Wussup wit' Tre Pound? I heard he got hit with another M."

Shelton told the guys he was with to stay put, then he cocked his head, signaling for Moses to follow him. They walked through the yard to somewhere private, where the east building casted a huge shadow on the field. There was a bench there. They sat on top of it and watched the other USP inmates jog the track.

"Tre Pound isn't a King anymore," Shelton said.

"Huh? Whaddaya mean?"

"He's been cut loose. I want you to know—because I know you and him are cool with each other—that anything he does from this point on in his life is not to be tied to the King name."

"What did he do? Did he snitch?"

"Yes. FBI has him on tape confessing that I murdered Drought Man. He also told Gutta, who was a confidential informant, that I killed Drought Man too. He told Gutta a lot of things he shouldn't have."

"I heard about Gutta snitching, but not Tre Pound. That's fucked up. I don't fuck wit' snitches, Shelton. If that's true, me and Tre Pound ain't cool no more."

"And that's not even the reason he's been disowned from the family."

"What else did he do?"

"He raped and murdered my little sister."

"Camille?!"

Shelton didn't respond. He was still watching the joggers. He didn't look upset, but Moses knew he was.

"I'm sorry to hear that," Moses said.

Shelton reached in the front pocket of his prison shirt and pulled out a couple cigars. He handed Moses one, and they lit up and talked about the charges Tre Pound got hit with and which ones got dismissed and evaded. Moses shared his info about his trafficking case and they both came to the conclusion that Tre Pound gave Gutta the scoop on the location where Moses was to meet his plug.

Essentially, Moses was here at USP because of Tre Pound.

"I need a favor," Shelton said.

Moses blew cigar smoke in the air. "What do you need me to do?"

"Just spread the word about Tre Pound," said Shelton. "Let the people you know who're in the State prison system know that Tre Pound is not a King. He's a rat and a rapist. He wants people to think highly of him, but I don't want the word *gangsta* to be attached to his name. I want his legacy to reflect what he is—a disloyal coward."

"I can do that. I'll tell everybody I know, I don't give a fuck."

"I wanted to apologize too," Shelton added, "for your girl Krystal getting entangled in my case. I heard the Feds caught her at my house and sent her to juvie. I feel responsible for that."

"Don't worry about it. That wasn't your fault. I blame that on the snitches."

Shelton gave Moses dap and got up and left. Moses still sat there and finished his cigar, thinking about how he and his once-loyal crew had fallen apart. Playa Paul, Stacks, Marlon, Tre Pound—they had a lot of fun and bizarre times and now it was over.

Moses took one last toke on the cigar and had to inspect its flaky fermented wrapping because it had a sweeter taste than the cigars they sold here in canteen. *Where the hell did Shelton get this?*

Tapping the cigar out on the table, Moses put it in his pocket to save it for later.

***

Toothpaste was like glue. Moses used it to tack a calendar on the wall in his cell. He cringed at the idea that he'd have to set up a new calendar nineteen more times after this.

A guard came to his cell. "You got a visit."

"Who is it?" Moses asked.

"I have no clue. They just told me to grab you."

Moses followed the guard out of the unit, wondering who was here to see him. He hadn't had a visit since he'd been here, and didn't expect to have one because he hadn't been in Leavenworth long and not too many family members knew he was here.

And really he didn't want a visit, didn't want to be reminded of a freedom that was too far off in the distance.

When he got to the visiting room the very thing he didn't want to happen started to happen. He started feeling homesick. There were girls in the visiting room—some halfway cute—that reminded him of girls he'd seen or passed by on the streets. And there was one lady near the back that he'd actually fuck. From where he stood, he could see she knew a little bit about style—a simple white blouse flowing over tight blue jeans that tucked into brown knee-high boots made her the best-dressed in the room. She was sitting next to a guy in a suit—her husband?— with her legs crossed, and around her neck was some kind of fancy Mardi Gras-looking jewelry. Moses imagined her standing on a high balcony flashing a group of drunken white boys for beads.

Stop fantasizing, Moses thought. *You got a 20-year sentence to do. Lust will get you nowhere.*

He looked around, trying to find his mother or auntie or anybody who looked familiar. His eyes fell on an older white man in a blue shirt and gray tie. The man looked like a detective, and he was staring directly at Moses.

Oh shit.

Moses walked over to the sergeant in charge of the visiting room. "Which one is my visit? I don't see nobody I know."

"Right over there, sir."

The sergeant pointed and Moses looked. The only people in that direction were the Mardi Gras girl and the suit next to her.

Curiously, Moses started heading that way, still thinking the guard was mistaken. But as he got closer he realized who the Mardi Gras girl was. It was Krystal!

And, strangely, sitting next to her was the super-lawyer Carlo Masaccio.

Moses started walking faster, and Krystal stood up and straightened out her blouse. His heart was thumping with overexcitement, and when he finally reached her he picked her up and spun her around several times. A guard had to tell him to put her down.

He hugged her, then kissed her passionately. When he finally let her go, he was flustered, in an excited feeling-lightheaded type of way. He shook Mr. Masaccio's hand.

"This is a helluva surprise!" Moses exclaimed, then sat down after they did. He leaned close and held Krystal's hands with a smile. "You look beautiful."

"And you look buffer." Krystal was grinning. "I like the new you."

"What are yall doing here? I mean, I'm out-of-my-mind happy to see you guys here, but what happened? Is everything okay?"

Mr. Masaccio spoke up. "My presence here might be scaring you a little bit but I assure you everything's fine. Mr. Shelton King asked me to bring your girlfriend here to reunite you two as soon as she was released. He felt responsible for Krystal's stay in juvenile and this is his attempt at making it right."

Moses shook the lawyer's hand again. "Thank you, sir. And I'm gonna show my thanks to Shelton somehow when I hit the yard again." He stared into Krystal's eyes. "Did you get my letters?" he asked.

"No. Camille never got a chance to send them off. And I found out why. She got murdered."

"I just heard the news this morning. I know Camille and Dominique were yo road dogs. Are you holding up okay?"

There was pain in Krystal's eyes, but she managed a small smile. "I'm doing better."

"I'm kinda glad you didn't get my letters. A couple of them got pretty mean. I thought you abandoned me."

She leaned closer to him, her shimmering necklaces hanging and clicking against each other. Her thumbs were massaging the tops of his hands. "I'm gonna be by your side forever. Me and you both have lost too many friends. We need each other."

Moses lifted her hand and kissed it. He thought about how Krystal's sudden presence would affect his incarceration. He'd probably be wondering about her day and night now, writing her constantly, waiting on pins and needles for return letters. He'd heard how stressful it could be.

But how he felt right now with her here—gratefully enthusiastic, alive, masculine, loved—made him feel like he was up for the challenge.

"This one visit is enough to last me ten years," Moses said.

"Be expecting many many more," she replied.

"Tell me about your time being locked up. I had faith in you, but I wasn't sure how well you'd survive."

Krystal rolled her eyes at the mention of her incarceration. "I made it, but OMG it sucked. Let me start by telling you about Tangie ..."

www.felonybooks.com

CPSIA information can be obtained at www.ICGtesting.com
Printed in the USA
LVOW06s2107090116

469907LV00001B/197/P